EDGE

A bitter Edge, remembering Wounded Knee. He was Captain Josiah Hedges then—officer in a war that turned father against son and brother against brother. It reduced men and women to the level of animals. It hung the shadow of death over a nation. And it gave Edge his first taste of killing . . . and betrayal.

Edge wasn't going to be betrayed again.

> **WARNING**
>
> This story is not for
> the faint-hearted reader.

EDGE:
HELL'S SEVEN

by
George G. Gilman

PINNACLE BOOKS • NEW YORK CITY

For
A.R.J.
and his fellow drummers
in the West
(as well as North, South and East)

Author's Note

This book relates the further adventures of Captain Josiah C. Hedges during the American Civil War. While the story is complete in itself, the reader's enjoyment may be enhanced if he first reads *Killer's Breed* and *Red River*.

Chapter One

THE SUN was at the midday peak of its height and intensity and nothing moved on the dusty floor of the wide valley between the brooding Sierras. An eerie silence clung to the cluster of buildings at its centre which seemed to be held prisoner in the shimmering heat mist by the dual silver threads of the railroad track, stretched in an arrow-straight line from one end of the valley to the other.

In an inky patch of shade from a rock overhang against the north facing side of a slab-like bluff, a man sat astride a roan mare and studied the desolate vista. He was a tall man—over six feet—and deceptively lean for his more than two hundred pounds was evenly distributed upon his frame and not a single ounce of it was excess fat. He wore a sweat-stained black shirt and Levis, dusty from a long ride, and tight-fitting enough to reveal the muscular development of his body. His face was poised on the borderline between handsomeness and ugliness so that the decision had to be made by the beholder. A fusion of Mexican and northern European blood had formed the features, so that clear blue eyes contrasted vividly with the dark coloration of skin stretched taut over high cheekbones. The whole was framed by thickly matted black hair which reached

9

from under a low-crowned black hat to brush the man's broad shoulders.

It was a face which, even in repose, looked incapable of expressing warmth and as the man looked out across the valley, narrowing his eyes to mere glinting slits and folding back his thin lips to emit a low whistling sound, a subtle hint of underlying cruelty could be seen in his features.

He was armed with an ageing Colt-Walker in a holster tied down to his right thigh and a Winchester rifle slid into the boot behind his saddle. He carried a third weapon but its presence was merely hinted at by a tell-tale bulge at his back, extending from under his hair and following the line of his spine for three inches. This bulging of his shirt was caused by a leather pouch containing a cut-throat razor.

The man on the roan mare was called Edge.

His survey completed, he heeled his mount forward, out into the burning heat of the sun, on a diagonal line towards the huddle of buildings. He held her down to a walk and appeared to be utterly at ease as he rode, straight in the saddle. But he was constantly alert, his hooded eyes sweeping the arid terrain, his right hand primed to claw for the pistol or rifle.

But he had covered a little more than three-quarters of the mile distance to the buildings before he heard a sound above his own regular breathing and the slap of the mare's hooves against the sun-baked ground. Edge did not break pace: simply concentrated his steady gaze upon the centre of the group of buildings, trying to recognise the origin of the sound. It was a gentle creaking noise, as if from a door swinging on neglected hinges in a wind. But the cadence was too steady and there was no wind today.

Edge steered his mount between two buildings, The Big Valley Saloon and the Big Valley Bank, to emerge upon a plaza. To the left and right it was flanked by a large house with an impressive verandah, and a church with a half-finished bell tower and a schoolhouse. The fourth side of the plaza was formed by a railroad track with the depot beyond. A sign proclaimed: BIG VALLEY STATION.

Every building except the church seemed to be complete in all respects save one—there were no people. The tiny town of Big Valley had been built and then immediately deserted, for there was about it an unmarred newness that bore no mark of habitation.

Edge showed no reaction to the strangeness of the town as he halted his horse in the centre of the plaza and raked his glinting eyes across the facades of the buildings. Then, when he had pinned down the direction from which the creaking sound came, he concentrated his scrutiny upon the cool shade of a doorway at the centre of the depot building.

'Come and set a spell, young feller,' a man invited easily, his voice croaky with age. 'Don't do a body no good being out in the sun like you are.'

Edge shaded his eyes with his hands, but was still able to see no further than the black rectangle of the open doorway. He rode a few more yards to the railroad tracks, then dismounted.

'Anyplace I can water the animal?' he asked.

11

The regular creaking continued. 'Ain't a drop to be had within twenty miles of here, young feller.'

Edge unhooked the canteen from the saddlehorn and shook it. It sounded no more than a quarter full. 'What time's the train due?'

'Goes through here at one. You come to watch her?'

Edge shook his head. 'Get on.'

A crackling sound came out of the depot and it took Edge a moment to realise the old man inside was laughing.

'I say something funny, mister?'

The man inside contained his gaffaws. 'You sure did, young feller. Ain't a train stopped here in Big Valley since the town was built. No need. Ain't nobody to get aboard and there sure ain't nobody wants to get off.'

Edge slid the Winchester from the saddle boot. 'Train'll stop today,' he said.

'Why's that, young feller?'

' 'Cause I want to get on it,' Edge answered easily, beginning to lead the mare across the track.

'Horseshit,' the old man croaked.

'Wrong—horsemeat,' Edge shot back, raised the Winchester and pumped a shell into the animal's brain.

As the horse sighed and rolled over onto its side across the track, the creaking sound ended abruptly.

Edge stepped up on to the planking of the depot and went through the doorway. 'Best she went quick,' he muttered. 'I seen animals die from lack of water.'

As his eyes became accustomed to the murky interior of the depot, Edge saw the old man sitting in the rocking chair. He was thin of body and wizen of face, dressed in a grey suit cut on city lines which had seen better days. His skin was crinkled and stained dark by the sun, emphasising the whiteness of his hair and the ragged moustache which decorated his upper lip. He submitted silently to the scrutiny and then began to rock back and forth in the chair as Edge moved his gaze to look at the room.

There were benches along two walls. A counter with a wire mesh shield partitioned off a third of the room. Over a square hole cut in the mesh was a sign which read: TICKETS. A large pile of crates were stacked in a corner. One of the crates had been dragged across and rested close to the rocker. All the bottles except one had been opened.

'Redeye,' the old timer croaked, reaching down a bony hand to draw the full bottle from the crate. 'What's a man need water for?'

The shade of the room was deceptive and the trapped heat served to emphasise the stale odour emanating from the old man.

'To maybe take a bath in,' Edge said with a grimace, advancing no further into the room.

The old timer uncapped the bottle and sucked at it noisily. 'I ain't one for the bathing,' he said. 'Name's Rose, young feller.'

'By any other name you'd smell as lousy,' Edge said, moving inside now, to sit on one of the benches. 'Depot manager?'

'I'm anything you want me to be in Big Valley. Today I'm depot manager 'cause there's a train

13

scheduled through. Ain't no train tomorrow. Maybe then I'll run the hotel, or act like a preacher at the church. Might even teach school. Ain't done that for a long time.'

Rose's voice sounded rational, but Edge realised he was either drunk or insane, perhaps both.

'You the only one who lives here?'

The old man's wrinkled face became sad. He nodded. 'Ain't the way I planned Big Valley when I built it. I figured to see streets being laid out from the plaza like spokes on a wheel. Weren't no gold in the hills, though. And there sure ain't enough rain in five years to make anything grow in the valley. So no reason why folks should move out here.'

Edge's impassive features showed no sympathy for the old man's shattered dream as he took out the makings. Rose apparently expected none, for he showed again that whatever he required could be extracted from a bottle of redeye.

'Like a drink, young feller?' he asked, holding out the bottle with spittle crawling down the neck.

Edge shook his head and lit the cigarette.

'Pleased of that. Last one I got.'

'Then what?' Edge asked with disinterest.

A fresh expression entered the bleary eyes and the ancient face showed something close to excitement. 'A man builds a town, he's got a right to destroy it.' He began to move the rocker again and the creaking sound restarted, as the runners curved down onto a loose floorboard. 'You reckon, young feller?'

'I reckon,' Edge replied.

The conversation lapsed and the only sounds in the tiny town came from the rocking of the chair

14

and the lazy buzzing of flies feeding upon the spilled blood of the dead horse. With the occasional wet noise of Rose sucking at the bottle.

But when a full thirty minutes had slipped by in the odorous, unmoving heat of the depot, each man content to be alone with his own thoughts, a new sound came in across the barren valley floor. Edge's expression did not alter as he listened and when he finally recognised the noise as that of a wagon and two-horse team, he confined his action to pumping a fresh shell into the breech of the Winchester.

'Hell, don't scare 'em off, young feller,' Rose said hurriedly. 'Big Valley ain't bin this busy since the construction crews left.'

The wagon was coming from the other side of the valley to where Edge had rode out of the mountains and had to bump across the track to enter the plaza. It was a flatbed with sides, driven by a young man. A woman, ten years his senior, rode as a passenger.

'Anybody around?' the man called anxiously as he brought the wagon to a halt.

Edge raised the canteen to his thin lips and studied the newcomers as he sipped at the tepid water. The man was, in fact, no more than a boy. He was about eighteen, standing two inches under six feet with a solid-looking, muscular body clothed in a brand-new, badly cut business suit. He wore no hat. His face was round, full of cheek and stubborn of jaw. His hair was the colour of old hay and seemed to be of the same texture, worn long in a fringe that stopped short of his anxious green eyes. As far as Edge could tell, the boy carried no gun.

15

'Come on in and set a spell, my boy,' Rose croaked in his standard greeting. 'And you, young lady.'

The woman matched her companion in height, but her build was thicker, generous with the curves of her sex which she exhibited proudly by wearing a white dress cut low at the front and hugging her tightly to the waist. Her long hair was jet black, falling to her shoulders from under the wide brim of her hat. The face in the deep shade of the brim was too long and angular to be pretty but there was about its structure, the set of her full lips and carefully applied make-up around her grey eyes, an unsubtle sensuality.

She moved with a forced elegance as the boy helped her down from the wagon. But the sight of the dead horse and the feeding flies upset her composure and a sudden lack of gracefulness marked her hurried progress across the track and into the depot. And the grimace that painted her face as she caught the smell of the old-timer cut across all she had learned about being a lady.

'Jesus Christ, what a stink!' she hissed, then shot a hurried, anxious glance over her shoulder to where the boy was taking two valises from the wagon.

Edge nodded to Rose. 'He ain't much for bathing.'

The woman seemed about to pass another acid comment, but checked herself as the boy thumped the bags down behind her and grinned into the depot. Rose nodded a greeting but Edge's cold expression did not waver.

'There's a dead horse on the track,' the boy said.

'They must know that, Alvin,' the woman replied

16

and her carefully modulated voice was as much a sham as the rest of her facade.

Rose sucked the last drop from the last bottle and slotted it into the crate. 'Young feller wants to get aboard the train. Good a way as any to stop her. Set yourselves down.'

Alvin looked at the woman and licked his lips. She nodded and allowed him to escort her to the bench that was vacant. When she was seated, she took off her hat and began to fan herself with it. Edge looked for long moments at the rising flesh of her breasts exposed above the dress, then dragged his gaze away to stare out into the harshly sunlit plaza. The creaking of the loose floorboard again became the only sound in the heated depot.

'Can we buy tickets here?' Alvin said at length.

'No sir,' Rose replied. 'Railroad company reckoned I had no right to build no depot, so they wouldn't grant me no franchise to sell tickets.'

Alvin looked confused. 'What do you think, Beth?' he asked.

'The conductor will have tickets, dear,' the woman replied.

'Come far?' Rose croaked.

Alvin bobbed his head. 'Redwood City, up north.'

'That's mighty far,' Rose agreed. 'More'n thirty mile, I reckon.'

Edge stood up and stretched. 'You won't be needing the team?'

Alvin shook his head. 'I guess not. I thought I'd sell them and the wagon here in Big Valley.'

A cackle of laughter spilled from under the old-timer's moustache. Edge ambled out into the plaza and stepped across the tracks. The two newcomers could not see him from where they sat and both started as the shots rang out.

'Don't look like he's got an ounce of kindness in him, does he?' Rose asked the couple. 'But he's a man with a feeling for horses. Don't want 'em to die of thirst.'

As Edge came to stand in the doorway, he was feeding three fresh shells into the Winchester's magazine. Alvin opened his mouth to speak, perhaps to protest. But Beth rested a hand on his arm and shook her head in warning.

A train whistle wailed, far off, and the sound had the timbre of an animal's plaintive cry.

'She's acoming, folks,' Rose said, pushing himself up out of the rocker and moving wearily towards the doorway, staggering only slightly from the effects of the whiskey.

Edge crossed to the ends of the planking beside the track and hooded his eyes to stare into heat shimmer at the western approach of the valley. A tiny black speck with a plume of smoke hovering above it appeared at the extremity of the track, where the twin gleam of the rails emerged into a single thread of silver.

Rose stepped ponderously over the track and angled across the plaza towards the broad stoop of the mansion. The couple stood behind Edge, the boy holding a valise in each of his smooth, hairless fists.

'Guess I should thank you for putting the animals out of their misery, mister,' he said. 'I ought to have done it. Only I don't carry a gun.'

The woman placed a proprietary grip on his coat

18

sleeve. 'I'm not marrying you because you're good with a gun, Alvin,' she assured the boy.

Edge turned a cold grin towards the woman, his narrowed eyes raking over her voluptuous body and settling for a few moments upon her sensuous features. Then he looked back along the track, to where the dot that was the locomotive had expanded and the smoke plume had darkened.

'A man's gotta do what a man can do best,' he muttered. 'One guy's meat is another man's Winchester 66.'

As Beth emitted an unladylike grunt of disgust, Edge continued to watch the approach of the train, recalling the last time he had ridden the railroad.

Chapter Two

THE engineer was a small, rotund man with round eyes in a round face. His eyes were black and his face was very white. He had been happy that morning, driving the big locomotive and its swaying passenger cars south through the sunlit undulations of eastern Georgia. So had his crewman. Both were in high spirits because the Southwestern Railroad did not often give raises and when the company showed beneficence, this was a cause for celebration.

It was the summer of 1863 and had either of the men been concerned with the Confederate cause in the bloody Civil War that gripped the nation, their moods would have been a great deal heavier. It had been a bad year for the South. In May, General Stonewall Jackson had died of gunshot wounds accidentally inflicted by his own men. In the same month Grant had begun his seige of Vicksburg which in July he captured, together with 30,000 Rebel troops. Port Gibson, Port Hudson and Gettysburg had also fallen to the Federal armies that year. True, Lee was moving north from Fredericksburg, launching a second invasion against the Yankee strongholds, but the omens were not good.

However, the ageing engineer and his younger colleague had no interest in the conflict. They operated their locomotive far from the battle zones and the closest they came to enemy troops was the daily halt at Anderson. And the wretched creatures fenced in behind the pine stockade and the cord marking the deadline of the nearby Andersonville Prison Camp posed no threat to the innocent employees of the railroad company.

Until that fine summer morning when Captain Josiah C. Hedges and six of his troopers broke free of the miserable squalor and killed the crewman as they commandeered the locomotive.*

Now, as the locomotive barrelled along at increasing speed, leaving the stranded passenger cars far behind, the full horror of war made itself known to the sweating engineer. Quaking before the controls, eyes glued to the pressure gauges, he was awesomely aware of what was happening behind him on the footplate. Two of his captors were dressed in ill-fitting grey uniforms. The other five wore the blue serge and gold insignia of Union cavalrymen, ragged and dirt-streaked from the long weeks of incarceration in the hellhole that was Andersonville.

One of the men in grey was an officer. He was the tallest of the escapers but like them he showed the signs of his harrowing experiences behind the stockade walls—hollowed out eye sockets, sunken cheeks and pallid skin resulting from the meagre prison regimen. The mere fact of being free and successfully stealing a train to speed them away from pursuit had, however, already begun to have an effect on the

*See—*Edge: The Blue, The Grey And The Red.*

22

men. A bouyancy of spirit injected hope into their minds and this was reflected in a strange lightness that emanated from their eyes as they drank in the sights of freedom.

The officer showed this least of all as he stood immediately behind the trembling engineer, studying the technique of driving the locomotive. And it was he whom the railroad man feared most. He seemed to be the only one who was armed—with a razor sheathed in a neckpouch which he could draw with lightning speed. And use with devastating effect, as he had revealed when he cold-bloodedly slit the throat of the crewman.

The man with the razor was Hedges. Behind him, cursing at the men to keep the firebox filled with logs, was Sergeant Frank Forrest, not quite so tall as the captain, but broader. He was the oldest of the men to break out of Andersonville and looked even meaner than Hedges when he cracked his lips to show crooked, tobacco-stained teeth.

The rest of the men were all in their early- to mid-twenties. The second man in Rebel grey was Hal Douglas who held the rank of corporal. Billy Seward, Roger Bell, John Scott and Bob Rhett were all troopers. With the exception of Rhett, the men had been moulded through the burning heat of countless battles into vicious machine-like creatures existing solely to kill the enemy, often each indistinguishable from another when the call to action came. Rhett was the exception because he had been born a coward and the terrors of war served only to darken the fear that was his constant companion.

23

'We going to get to any spur that'll loop us north?' Hedges roared in the engineer's ear.

They had been speeding southwards for more than a mile and the sudden question caused the engineer to start. He looked over his shoulder and found his gaze captured by the slitted blue eyes of Hedges, contrasting so oddly with the Mexican cast to the rest of his lean features. He shook his head emphatically. 'Not 'till we hit Valdosta close by the Florida state line, mister. And we ain't got firing and water enough to get that far.'

'Christ, Captain!' Forrest roared. 'We're goin' like a bat outa hell. But we ain't gettin' no place.'

Hedges raised a dark-skinned hand and jerked the engineer's attention back to the controls. Then he turned to treat Forrest to a cold grin. 'I'm open to suggestions, Sergeant,' he called.

Forrest was a man ill-fitted for army discipline with its chains of command. He had come to the war after many years of bounty hunting in the south-western territories, where he had always been the one to give the orders and make the plans. But he had learned to comply with Hedges' commands by gaining respect for the Captain: not as an officer but as a man—the first one he had ever met who he considered to be smarter than himself.

Hedges was aware of this; just as he knew that the other five men who had always been the nucleus of his Troop would continue to follow his orders only for as long as the relationship between their captain and their sergeant was maintained at the *status quo*. He was certain, as he had been from the very moment these men thrust themselves upon him on a scarred battlefield*, that Forrest could not be allowed to win the most minor confrontation. For if he did the group would degenerate into a vicious mob, ready to kill without purpose or profit. And although, on occasion, Hedges himself lost sight of the cause for which he was fighting, he could not condone bloodshed for its own sake.

Thus, alongside the battle he waged against the Rebels, the Captain had a constant struggle to contain his sergeant, who periodically chose to test his superiority. Because Hedges wanted earnestly to retain the group as a fighting unit—not out of respect for them as soldiers, but because he regarded the troopers as killers of a very special breed. And killing the enemy to win the war was his prime objective.

Forrest was taken by surprise at the invitation, unable to conjure up an instant plan to get them out of their predicament. But, as the men looked at him expectantly, he cracked a crooked-toothed grin. 'What's up, Captain? Running out of ideas?'

Hedges shook his head and shot a glance along and then back down the track. 'Just time, Sergeant,' he answered.

The men, resting from the onerous task of feeding logs to the fire, glanced suspiciously out at the countryside through which the locomotive was speeding. The wasteland of denuded pine woods and fallow cottonfields in the vicinity of the prison camp had been left behind. Now they were amid a rolling wilderness of untilled meadows and gentle hills cov-

*See—*Edge: Killer's Breed.*

ered with cypress and pine in which the railroad was the sole sign of man's encroachment upon nature. It looked tranquil in the warm morning sunlight, but foremost in each man's mind was the knowledge that Georgia was enemy territory.

'You reckon they'll come after us?' Seward asked of anybody who cared to answer.

'You see any goodwill committee waving us off, lunkhead?' Scott yelled.

'She's goin' fit to bust her boiler now,' the engineer put in nervously, his gaze glued to the steam gauge as the needle crept towards the danger mark.

Hedges peered ahead, narrowing his eyes against the slipstream pressure. 'I don't see any telegraph line?'

The engineer shook his head. 'Ain't one across this stretch of country, Mister Captain, sir.'

'So we just gotta worry about the guys behind us,' Scott drawled, and grinned at Rhett. 'All of us 'cepting Rhett, of course.'

The comment raised strained smiles on the faces of some of the men. Rhett was a blatant fag.

Hedges did not react to the humour as he leaned across in front of the engineer, who leapt away in fear. The Captain's fist clenched around the control level and eased it away from full throttle. The straining locomotive continued to race along the track at its maximum speed and then began to slow down.

'Wrong way!' the engineer yelled anxiously.

'Forrest!' Hedges snarled, applying the brakes to decrease the headlong rush even more.

26

'Captain?'

'Casey Jones has anything more to say, put him in the firebox. Head first.'

Forrest grinned at the wide-eyed engineer and the rotund little man let out a gasp and pressed himself back against the side of the cab.

The wheels intermittently screeched and showered sparks as Hedges applied and released the brakes and, when the locomotive rounded a curve at the foot of a hillock and plunged through a cutting in a cypress grove, he shut off the steam completely and hauled hard on the lever. With an angry hissing and a drawn-out, high-pitched shriek of protest, the locomotive slithered to a halt.

The men looked nervously into the trees on either side and then back to where the gleaming rails went from sight around the hillock.

'We forgot to bring the picnic hamper,' Rhett muttered in his cultured New England tones.

'I heard roasted Rebel's good to eat,' Seward answered, grinning evilly at the quivering engineer, whose round eyes implored Hedges to give him protection.

He was about to proclaim his lack of support for the Confederate cause, but as he saw the impassive expression on the Captain's face, he recalled the warning.

'Ain't lunchtime yet,' Hedges said evenly, watching the black wood smoke that continued to belch from the inverted cone of the funnel. 'How'd we kill that, Casey? You can talk now.'

The engineer had to fight a lump back down from

27

his throat. 'You gotta damp it down,' he finally croaked.

'Wrong,' Hedges answered. '*You* gotta damp it down. Do it.'

The man moved forward to comply and the troopers eyed Hedges expectantly.

'End of the line, uh Captain?' Bell asked.

Hedges nodded curtly. 'Forrest: take Seward, Douglas and Bell into the trees on the right. Scott and Rhett, over to the left.'

The troopers complied without question, Forrest holding back only long enough to take down the sledge hammer from its brackets at the side of the cab. Hedges glanced to left and right, seeing the thick foliage sway back into place after the men had plunged into the trees.

Steam had ceased to hiss from the piston valves and the plume of smoke was noticeably losing its density. The sweating engineer worked frantically to complete his task. He was awesomely aware of the hard-faced Captain towering above him.

'You gonna kill me, Mister Captain, sir?' he blurted out when he could take the tense silence no longer.

'You do anything except run a locomotive and gab?' Hedges snarled.

'Please, I gotta wife and six young 'uns,' the engineer implored as the final veil of smoke rose and disintegrated in the hot, unmoving air.

'Too much screwing don't guarantee a man a long life,' Hedges responded coldly. 'Into the trees, Casey.'

As the man climbed down from the footplate on the side indicated by Hedges, his mind raced, seeking a reason that might keep him alive. 'I know Georgia like the back of my hand!' he blurted out as Hedges shoved him between the trees when Scott and Rhett had gone from sight.

The two troopers were crouched in a patch of flattened undergrowth. Hedges checked that the spot offered a view of the stationary locomotive through a tracery of screening leaves and nodded his satisfaction.

Rhett's vapidly handsome face was run with the sweat of fear. 'What if there's a whole trainload of them, Captain?' he whispered.

'He's chicken again, Captain,' Scott said scornfully.

'So he ought to know not to count them before they hatch,' Hedges replied curtly, then raised his voice. 'Forrest?'

'Yeah?' came an answering call from the other side of the locomotive.

'I figure just as many as they can get aboard a loco. Won't want it slowed down by any cars.'

'If the Rebs are that smart,' Forrest called back.

'Move as soon as it hits.'

'You bet.'

'You want any prisoners, Cap?' Seward yelled.

'Crazy lunkhead,' Forrest snarled, loud enough to carry across the railroad, avoiding the necessity for Hedges to respond.

Silence settled upon the sunlit grove and was maintained for several minutes as the men crouched in their respective groups on each side of the deserted locomotive. But then their breathing quickened and became loud as straining ears picked up the distant rumble of an approaching locomotive.

'Sounds like a Camelback,' the engineer whispered, airing his knowledge.

'Any cars?' Hedges rasped, his hand flashing to the back of his neck and drawing the open razor.

Fear leapt across the round face, then the man leaned forward, concentrating upon the expanding volume of sound, certain his life depended upon giving the correct estimate.

'Come on, come on,' Hedges urged, his hooded eyes boring into those of the engineer as the track began to hum with the vibration of the approaching locomotive.

The man shook his head. 'Not a one,' he shouted above the thud of racing pistons.

'Be here when we get back,' Hedges snapped and stood up.

Scott and Rhett sprang to their feet behind him.

The engineer had called it correctly. The ungainly-looking Camelback roared around the curve unencumbered by cars. Two grey clad infantrymen clung to the front, two more above the tanks on each side and there were half a dozen crowded on the footplate with the two crewmen.

The hillock had obscured the stationary locomotive until there was less than four hundred feet before impact. And this was not enough. The braking wheels locked and scalding steam gushed from outlets. The Union troopers could see every line of desperate horror inscribed upon the faces of the Rebels, but the full throated screams were swamped by the clamorous din of the slithering locomotive as it raced towards the inevitable collision.

Two men hurled themselves from the footplate, to be smashed against the ends of the ties, their broken bodies tumbling like rag dolls along the sides of the track.

Then the shattering impact came.

As Scott raced from cover to snatch up the carbines dropped by the dead men, the Camelback crunched into the rear of the empty locomotive. The cabin of the stationary loco crumpled as if it were made of cardboard a moment before the force of the crash sent the engine forward, to topple sideways off the track.

The Camelback started to rear like a crazed horse, its crushed front end glistening with the moist red pulp which was all that remained of the two Rebels who had been clinging there. Then it seemed to be trying to right itself, the leading wheels dipping for the tracks. But the rails had been buckled and the wheels sheared into the ties.

Men were flung from the footplate, their screams of agony driven into silence by the harsh grinding of metal against metal. Hot cinders from the firebox and scalding steam from a broken valve spewed out after the men, exploding their clothes into flames and searing the skin from their faces.

The Camelback teetered on the brink, then slammed over on to its side, squelching the gore from the two Rebels clinging to the tank: catapulting the two from the other side to a crushing death against inanimate tree trunks.

All movement of both locomotives was finished in

seconds but the angry death rattle of escaping steam continued to hiss from the Camelback as the Union troopers broke from cover to search for undamaged weapons and supplies of ammunition. The engineer ignored them, staring in stunned silence at the jagged and crumpled metal of the wreckage—like a man paying his last respects to dead colleagues.

A glance was enough to convince Hedges that no one had survived the wreck, but Forrest circled the Camelback with a fixed grin of evil on his face and the sledge hammer swinging easily in one hand. But as he stared down at each broken body and found no movement the light of hate in his pig-like eyes became dulled by frustration. The stink and the humiliation of Andersonville was still clinging to him and the need for revenge was a broiling fury inside him.

As he stared down into the blackened face of the final victim and caught the sickly sweet odour of burned flesh, the rage exploded. His ear-splitting bellow drew all eyes in his direction. Then he grasped the sledge hammer in both hands, raised it high and pounded it downwards.

The hammer head thudded home in the area of the man's nose and sank deep into the flesh of his face. Blood and bone fragments splashed upwards.

'We only have to kill them once, Sarge,' Douglas yelled.

Forrest drew in a deep breath and let it out as a long sigh. Then he shot an expectant glance towards Hedges.

'Andersonville's still there, Forrest,' the Captain said softly.

Forrest nodded and hurled the hammer at the

32

overturned Camelback. 'But I ain't in it no more, Captain.'

'And it ain't in you, either?'

'Right.'

The men finished gathering up enough serviceable weapons to arm each with a rifle and a revolver—Spencers and Colts—and a supply of ammunition.

The engineer watched the men, terror at his own fate replacing the horror of the carnage.

'Ain't a decent uniform among 'em, sir,' Scott reported after circling the wreck. 'All either ripped to shreds or soaked in blood.'

Hedges acknowledged this with a shake of his head and slitted his eyes to look up at the sun. He pointed towards the brow of the hillock. 'Due north's that way,' he declared flatly. 'Which is the way we'll go. Casey, you'll lead us—and tell me what's up ahead every time I ask you.'

The engineer bobbed his head and wiped sweat from his forehead. 'Yes, sir, Mister Captain.'

'First off we need a place not too far from here where we can rest up 'till dark.'

'An' get somethin' to eat?' Bell suggested.

'What you want, a goddam hotel?' Forrest snarled at him.

'Man's gotta eat to live,' Bell said in a whining tone.

'Breathing's more important,' Hedges put in. 'Let's move out before the Rebs start to get anxious and we get more company.'

The group circled the wrecked locomotives, now silent and mournful with their attendant scattering of broken and twisted bodies. They moved into the trees and started up the slope in ranks of two, led by Hedges and the engineer.

'What a way to ruin a railroad,' Rhett murmured as he took a final look back at the scene of the smash. 'Just as I was starting to feel like a real railroad man.'

'You ain't lost the chance, Bob,' Scott replied with an obscene leer. 'Maybe the Captain will let you have Casey Jones when he's through with him.'

'You know I didn't mean . . .' Rhett began to respond.

'Cut out the yakking,' Hedges hissed.

Scott winked at the fag and lowered his voice to a whisper. 'Guess wartime ain't a gaytime.'

* * *

A RED glow showed behind the windows of the big house as the engineer spotted the horse carcase blocking the track and clamped on the brakes. Edge, Alvin and Beth watched the sparks flying from the locked wheels, then glanced across the plaza as the drunken old-timer came down off the stoop and made ungainly haste towards the bank.

A pane of glass cracked and a tongue of flame licked hungrily at the air outside.

'He's burning the town!' Alvin exclaimed, switching his startled gaze to the opaque glass window of the bank as it took on an orange hue.

'He must be crazy,' Beth said.

Edge spat onto a tie. 'Thirsty,' he corrected. 'He ran out of whiskey.'

'That's no reason,' the woman responded angrily

34

as Rose staggered out of the bank and waved cheer-fully towards the trio before entering the saloon.

The train came to a grinding halt, the big cow-catcher at the front of the locomotive nudging the dead roan mare.

'Dry town's no use to a man like him,' Edge said, and started along the side of the locomotive, noisy with pent-up power.

'What's going on here?' the engineer shouted, his sweating face purple with anger. 'Who put that animal on the track?'

Edge halted and stared up at the footplate, narrowing his eyes and curling back his lips. 'I heard you didn't figure to stop at Big Valley.'

'Damn right,' the engineer shot back. 'You coulda killed people.'

Edge shifted the Winchester from his shoulder and held it across the front of his body, the gesture just short of a threat. 'I ain't lost the chance,' he said easily.

'Hey, Lou, the whole town's on fire!' the crewman yelled excitedly.

As the two men stared around them, seeing smoke and flames billowing from the buildings on three sides of the plaza, Edge moved casually away, along the side of the train. Beth walked sedately behind him as Alvin struggled to keep up, panting from the strain of carrying the baggage.

Cursing, half in anger and half in fear, the crew-men leapt down from the footplate and struggled to haul the dead horse off the track. A broad spectrum of expressions showed upon the faces of the passen-gers as they looked out through the car windows on

35

to the trio seeking seats. They ranged from irritation at the delay of the unscheduled halt, through curiosity and indifference to a series of broad grins. These last decorated the round, sallow faces of about a dozen Chinese who occupied a car in the centre of the line.

' 'Bye, folks!' Rose yelled from the front of the train as he came out of the depot amid a cloud of smoke. 'Have yourselves a good trip.'

'Utterly mad,' Beth muttered as Edge stepped up on to the car platform.

'As a March Hare,' Alvin agreed, glaring at Edge's back as he was forced to set down the valises in order to help the woman up the steps.

Flames were supplementing the heat of the sun from all four sides of the plaza now and sparks, with no wind to carry them, began to float down over the train. The breathless crewmen had to concede defeat as the dead weight of the carcase refused to shift an inch.

'Come on,' the engineer rasped at length. 'Have to try and shunt the damn thing outta the way.'

He raced back to the footplate and climbed aboard, the fireman hard at his heels.

Back in the centre car, Edge lowered himself onto an aisle seat beside one grinning Chinese and facing two more. Alvin and Beth had to go to the far end of the car to locate two seats together. The train strained, jerked, rattled and inched forward. The dead horse was pushed along on the track for a few feet, then canted to the side and rolled clear. The train picked up speed and the passengers stared out in amazement at the raging flames which had now taken a strong grip on the tinder dry buildings.

'Big Valley a good town to be leaving, sir.'

Edge looked at the man sitting directly opposite him. Like all the other Chinese positioned through the car, he was in his mid-twenties, small of stature, with a smooth, clean-shaven face and blank eyes untouched by his smile. Also in common with his fellow countrymen, he wore a straw coolie hat and a loose-fitting, ankle-length robe the colour of a thundercloud with capacious sleeves concealing his hands on his lap.

'I think things get too hot for the gentleman,' the man beside Edge said.

Laughter rattled in the throat of the third Oriental. Edge remained impassive.

'Look, Miss Gertrude!' a man exclaimed in the seat behind Edge, pointing a trembling finger across the plaza. 'There's a man on the church roof.'

Edge joined all the other passengers in turning his eyes towards the stumpy, half-finished tower of the church. The figure of Rose could be seen amid the billowing black smoke as the old-timer clung to a support strut and waved at the departing train with his free hand.

'My God, Mr. Stein!' a woman shrieked. 'He's going to jump.'

A series of gasps rippled through the car as the man who had built Big Valley took a final look around at its destruction and plunged head-first into the blazing church.

'Whatever makes a man do such a thing?' the woman's companion asked.

'He was one of a generation that lost out,' Edge muttered as he moved into a more comfortable position in the seat and pulled his hat brim low over his eyes. 'Rose ain't Rose ain't Rose no more.'

The train steamed out of the town and picked up speed, racing away from the angry flames and the listless plumes of smoke. And as the wheels settled into a regular rhythm of noise and the cars began to sway smoothly, Edge allowed his mind to rove back into time again.

Chapter Three

THE section of Georgia through which the engineer led Hedges and the troopers had never been densely populated but now, at the height of the war, the country was almost deserted. The group had to move in a wide circle to avoid a tiny hamlet but was able to cut straight across a number of farmsteads and plantations which had been abandoned by women whose menfolk had gone away to fight and been reported missing or killed.

It was at one of these sadly derelict farms that the Captain called a halt. The sun was nearing its noon peak and the men were tired and irritable after an arduous march which had taken them far away from the blood-soaked wreckage at the railroad. Added to the strain of starved bodies forced to press forward at a fast pace through the harsh heat was the necessity, constantly stressed by Hedges, for the men to cover their tracks. Thus, each twig that was broken and every footprint made in a patch of soft earth had to be systematically concealed or obliterated. And hunger was a further contributing factor to the men's exhaustion as they collapsed in the shaded coolness of the bare living room in the tiny farmhouse.

Of the group, the overweight engineer should

have finished the trek with a degree of freshness, but his ever-present fear of the escaped prisoners-of-war served to reduce him to the same level of weariness as the others.

'Jesus!' Seward breathed as he sank to the floor in one corner, resting his back into the angle of the walls. 'And some crazy coot had the nerve to write a song about marching through Georgia.'

Forrest leaned against the high mantel above the crumbling brick fireplace and scowled at the men as they sank to the floor, some of them taking off their boots and massaging aching feet.

'Just look at the cruds, Captain,' he snarled. 'Spend months sitting on their asses and keel over soon as they take a little stroll.'

Hedges was at the window, looking out through the cracked pane at the flat landscape stretching westwards at the front of the house. 'You're so fresh, Sergeant, you stand first watch at this window,' he replied. They had approached the house from the rear and he knew that the terrain in that area was slightly broken, featured with a few stands of oak and pine trees. He jerked his rifle towards the open door to the kitchen. 'Seward, take the window at the back. Wake Douglas and me after two hours. After us, Bell and Scott will take over.'

Seward groaned. 'Aw, what about Bob, Captain?' he whined.

'Guess Rhett's excused duty,' Scott muttered. 'Maybe he's feeling queer.'

The men's laughter had a hollow ring, as if indulgence in humour required as much effort as anything else. Hedges' face was impassive as he regarded the facile handsomeness of the New Englander.

'I don't want him screaming like a stuck pig if he so much as sees a jack rabbit move outside,' the Captain said flatly. 'Rhett, you'll make sure Casey Jones don't get itchy feet.'

Rhett was insulted, then anxious. 'How will I do that and get some sleep?' he pleaded, looking from Hedges to the nervous engineer and back again.

Hedges stretched out on the bare boards of the floor close to the door and closed his eyes. But although his posture suggested relaxation, his right hand maintained a tight grip on the Spencer repeater. His voice was already drowsy as he replied: 'You had a college education, Rhett. Use your initiative.'

The men not detailed for duty lost no time in following Hedges' example and within a minute the sounds of ragged breathing and heavy snoring filled the room. During this time, Rhett treated the engineer to a steady, hateful stare which drove the fat little man closer and closer to the brink of babbling terror. Then, for a few moments, the man had time to gather his wits as Rhett rose and wandered about the room, opening and closing doors. When the New Englander found one which opened on to the room he wanted, he jerked his Colt at the engineer.

'Into the kitchen, bastard,' he hissed.

The engineer began to quake again as he stepped over the sleeping men to comply with the order.

Forrest did not turn away from his surveillance of the sunlit countryside. His voice was a weary drone.

41

'If you're gonna cook him, Rhett, don't give me no cuts off the rump.'

'What you gonna do?' the engineer stuttered.

Like the worst cowards, Rhett was able to put on a veneer of toughness when he had a victim at his mercy. His right hand rammed forward and the engineer bent double, the breath whooshing out of him as the Colt muzzle stabbed into his bulbous stomach.

'Ask no questions and you'll get told no lies,' Rhett said harshly, hooking a slim hand around the man's thick neck and jerking him forward into the kitchen. He went in after him and closed the door.

The only movement within the range of vision of either Forrest or Seward was the almost inperceptible slide of the sun down the western blue of the sky. For the heat level did not fall and seemed to induce a lethargy even in the creatures whose natural habitat was in the overgrown fields around the house.

Hedges and Douglas stood their guard in identical circumstances and not until Bell and Scott were halfway through their duty did a cooling breeze waft in from the east. Stirred up by the rustling of leaves, small animals began to scurry through the long, parched grass and crickets started an incessant commentary of their presence.

At six o'clock, when a bank of grey cloud had formed along the western horizon and began to spread across the sky by the minute, heralding an early twilight, Hedges woke up and roused the other three men who had been sleeping.

During each change-over of sentry duty, nobody had asked the whereabouts of Rhett and his charge.

But as the men licked dry lips with parched tongues and made no effort to staunch the rumbling of empty stomachs, Hedges voiced the question.

'In there,' Forrest replied, jerking a thumb towards the kitchen door.

Hedges nodded to Douglas who used the stock of his rifle to push open the door. The Union corporal in Confederate grey grinned.

'Got another song for you, Billy. Homo on the range.'

The men crowded around the doorway and looked with amusement across the stone floor of the kitchen, to where Rhett was stretched out on the wide stove with his head resting on the edge of the sink. He was snoring gently. Then their attention was captured by a series of muffled grunts and they saw the engineer. He was hanging in a closet, his feet some eighteen inches above the ground, with a meat hook piercing each shoulder of his denim coveralls and sunk into a beam. His hands were tied behind his back and his mouth was gagged. His round eyes seemed to bulge from his head in a silent plea for release.

'Guy looks hung up over Rhett,' Seward said.

'Get him off the hook,' Hedges ordered, and scowled at the sleeping man. 'And wake up dreaming boy.'

As Scott and Bell moved across to release the engineer, Seward closed in on Rhett. He leaned down to place his mouth against the ear of the sleeping man.

'Boo!' he said harshly.

Rhett came awake in a cold sweat and started to quake.

'Company, sir!' Forrest hissed from the living room.

'Keep him gagged,' Hedges snapped, pointing to the engineer, then turning and creeping along the wall to where Forrest was crouched by the front window.

The Captain ducked low and scuttled to the other side of the aperture. He peered out into the gathering early dusk and clicked his tongue against the back of his teeth as he saw the group of horsemen in a cautious approach to the house.

'At least ten,' Hedges said.

'And two more,' Forrest answered, bringing up his rifle. 'But they ain't got a brain between 'em. First saw 'em, they were fanned out real good. Closer they come, more they bunched. First shot into the middle ought to take out at least four of 'em.'

'And make holes in their uniforms,' Hedges said with a shake of his head. 'Maybe scare off the horses, too.' He looked back into the room, at the men crouched there. Rhett had reassumed responsibility for the engineer and was pressing a Colt into the side of the man's neck. 'Douglas, cover the rear. Nobody get trigger happy.' He returned his attention to the Rebel cavalry patrol. 'What's their ranking?' he asked of Forrest.

The Sergeant showed the Captain his crooked grin. 'You wanna stay a Johnnie Reb, sir, you get demoted. Top man's a lieutenant. Then there's two sergeants and a corporal. Rest are enlisted men.'

Hedges' hooded eyes examined the enemy soldiers as they halted their horses some three hundred feet in front of the house. Their faces were mere areas of

44

paleness against the dark grey of their uniforms and caps. But the apprehension of some of the group could be seen in the way rifle barrels were levelled and hands dropped to holstered side arms.

'Anybody in there?' a man at the head of the group called. His voice was young, holding a timbre of nervousness.

'Come in and find out, why don't you?' Seward breathed.

'I reckon we oughta pour some lead in there, Lieutenant,' an older voice growled.

'The man's a sadist,' Rhett said softly.

More voices sounded from the group, but too low to carry as far as the house. Then two men slid from their saddles and, with rifles levelled at the ready, moved cautiously forward. Hedges ducked back under the window and stabbed a finger at Forrest, Seward and Scott—finally at the bedroom door. The men moved forward to join Douglas who was guarding the window in there. Then the Captain indicated that the rest of the men should go into the kitchen.

'All we want is the drop on them,' he hissed as he crossed the threshold.

Both doors were pushed almost closed. The two Confederate cavalrymen had covered half the distance to the house, their eyes and ears straining to pick up a sign of danger. In the bedroom Douglas continued to crouch by the window as Forrest, Seward and Scott stood in an arc to one side of the door. In the kitchen, taking his cue from Hedges, Bell helped to hoist the quaking engineer back onto the hooks in the closet.

45

Because of his tallness, Hedges' head was on almost the same level as that of the hanging man. He leaned close to him. 'Soon as they come in, make a racket,' he whispered.

The man's eyes grew wider, as if in disbelief. Hedges treated him to a cold grin and nodded. Then, with three silent strides, he reached the rear door and pulled it open. He jerked his head and Bell and Rhett followed him outside. He closed the door and pressed his finger against his thin lips as Douglas looked at him in amazement from the bedroom window. Then he motioned for Bell to go to one corner of the house before leading the anxious Rhett to the other.

The two Rebel soldiers, sweating from the strain, reached the house and flattened themselves against the wall on each side of the front door. They paused a moment, then one of them lifted his foot and launched a back-heeled kick at the door. It crashed open. They leapt into the opening, bringing up their rifles. Their sighs of relief echoed in the empty room.

Then fear clawed cold fingers around their throats again as the engineer began to moan through his gag and kick his feet against the sides of the closet. The men rushed across the room and adopted the same tactics as they employed at the front door.

'Jesus, will you look at that!' the taller of the two exclaimed as he saw the frantically struggling form of the engineer.

'They must have been here,' the other shot back. 'Them's railroad man's threads. Get him down while I call the lieutenant.'

The engineer began to struggle with greater vigour

and the veins stood out in his face and neck as he tried to warn his rescuers of danger. But the tall cavalryman chose to set him free of the hooks before taking off the gag. And the second man hurried out to the front door.

'They been, but they've gone, Lieutenant!' he yelled. 'Left the engineer here though.'

The rest of the patrol heeled their horses forward, still bunched together, heading for the house. Hedges waited until the enemy soldiers were lost to sight around the angle of the house and, after beckoning to Bell, led Rhett along the wall. At the front corner he held back, listening to the sounds of the men dismounting and going inside. Then, after a glance around the angle, he motioned for Rhett to hold the horses. He signalled to Bell at the other corner and both men crept towards the open front door, Bell having to duck below the level of the window sill. They paused, Hedges nodded: they stepped into the opening and across the threshold, rifles cocked and levelled.

'They're here!' the engineer screamed from the kitchen.

'Ain't that the truth,' Hedges said evenly into the shocked silence which followed the shout.

The eleven men trying to crowd into the kitchen doorway whirled around, jostling each other to draw a bead on the two Union men. Hedges raised the Spencer and squeezed the trigger. The roar of the shot had a freezing effect on the Rebels. The man whose head was showered with wood splinters and plaster from the ceiling did not even blink.

'There's only two of 'em, sir,' an old sweat growled.

47

Hedges shook his head, his lips curling back to show his teeth in an evil grin. 'Wrong,' he chided. 'Count them.'

The frightened eyes of the Rebels swivelled to the bedroom door as it creaked open and Forrest came into view, followed by Seward, Douglas and Scott, each with a rifle cocked and aimed. And each with a brittle grin veneering his emaciated features. The six Union men formed a half circle around the cluster of Rebels.

With the exception of the old sweat, the patrol was composed of fresh-faced youngsters hardly out of their teens. The officer seemed to be among the youngest.

'The report I received specified seven escapers,' the lieutenant said, having to force his voice to maintain a level tone.

'Rhett's our ace in the hole,' Hedges answered.

'Asshole, more like,' Seward muttered.

'We still got 'em almost two to one,' the veteran complained.

'Guy's got a big mouth,' Forrest growled.

'Don't match his build, though,' Hedges pointed out. 'He don't size up to any of us.'

Forrest shot a glance at the Captain and licked his lips. 'You mean I can . . .?'

'Might convince these guys to toss their guns into the corner,' Hedges allowed, nodding towards the area he had in mind.

'You got anything else to say, big mouth?' Forrest demanded, glaring at the leather-like features of the oldest Rebel.

'Go to hell!' the man retorted.

48

'After you,' Forrest answered as his Spencer exploded.

The old sweat took the .52 calibre shell in the throat, the impact smacking him back against the wall. His legs folded under him and he toppled sideways.

The men's eyes showed tacit pleas for guidance from the lieutenant. The young officer dragged his shocked gaze away from the gaping wound in the dead man's throat and struggled to find his voice.

'You'll guarantee the safety of my men?' he asked hoarsely.

'They'll get treated like lambs,' Hedges answered tonelessly.

The lieutenant nodded, and threw his rifle into the corner indicated by Hedges. Then he unfastened his ammunition belt with its attached holster and tossed this in the same direction. When all the men were disarmed, Forrest moved forward and relieved the dead Rebel of his pistol and rifle, adding them to the pile.

The evening was giving birth to the new night now and in the gloom invading the room the pale faces of the Rebels were distrustful. But the most frightened man of all was the fat little engineer who had jostled himself into the centre of the group.

'What now?' the lieutenant asked.

'Strip,' Hedges answered.

Several of the men gasped.

'What?' The lieutenant swallowed hard.

'You heard him, and he outranks you,' Forrest snapped. 'You want me to blast some more little 'uns, Captain?'

Hedges spat at a beetle crawling across the floor. He missed. 'Give them three seconds.'

Before Forrest could open his mouth to start counting, the men were fumbling at their tunic buttons.

'Me, too, Mister Captain, sir?' the trembling engineer stuttered.

'You're sweating so much, Casey, I reckon you'll be doing yourself a favour.'

The little man hurried to take off his coveralls.

'Just the uniforms, caps and boots,' Hedges intoned as several of the men began to pull off their underwear. 'Rhett might be peeking and we wouldn't want to get him excited.'

Looking even more defenceless in their state of undress, clustering closer together as if for protection, the Rebels stared dejectedly as each of their six captors stooped down from the half circle of guards to select and don a uniform and then pick out an ammunition belt. The best fits provided Hedges and Bell with the rank of sergeants and the others were kitted out as privates. A spare trooper's uniform was selected for Rhett.

'Grey never was my colour,' Seward complained. 'Only reason I joined the Union army instead of the Johnnie Rebs.'

'Take their guns out and dump them!' Hedges ordered, snapping his gaze from Seward to Douglas.

Nobody said anything else until the task had been completed, which entailed two trips by each man. The beetle made another trek across the dusty floor. The heel of one of Hedges' newly-acquired boots crushed it.

'Obliged for your help, Lieutenant,' the Captain said, backing towards the door. 'We'll need seven of your horses as well.'

'But lambs we don't need,' Forrest pointed out.

Hedges shrugged. 'So give them the chop.'

His was the first shot, crashing into the chest of the young lieutenant. The man stumbled backwards, spraying his blood across the grubby underwear of his troopers. Screams and sobs rent the near darkness that had come to the room. The helpless Confederate soldiers, with the frantic engineer in their midst, clawed at each other in an attempt to force entrance to the kitchen. But then the other Union men began to fire into the panicked group, each explosion heralding another scream which was instantly swamped by more gunshots.

Blood gushed from countless wounds in the heads and bodies of the Rebels as one lifeless form after another was added to the heap of carnage. Bone, flesh and blood spattered against the wall and door. The wide-eyed dead stared through the gloom into the hate-crazed faces of their killers. In the silence which followed the slaughter, gunsmoke added an acrid taint to the hot air.

'Guess Andersonville ain't in any of us no more,' Forrest snarled.

'And those bastards sure won't be sending any Yankees to that hell-hole,' Seward snarled.

Another shot reverberated in the foul-tasting air and as the six men whirled towards the door, six more followed the first. Rhett's sallow face was carved in a mask of savagery as he emptied his Spencer. Each

51

bullet made a dull plop as it drilled through the dead flesh.

Forrest sighed. 'Like the man said, Bob, once is enough.'

'I was in that lousy place, too,' the New Englander responded spitefully.

'Where are the horses?' Hedges demanded.

'Tied up, Captain,' Rhett answered. 'Safe.'

Hedges nodded curtly and motioned for Rhett to shed his tattered Union garb and don the spare uniform. Then the men moved out into the clean-smelling darkness and took their pick of the horses. Water canteens and rations from the saddlebags were shared equally under the Captain's supervision. They ate as they rode.

'Pity about Casey gettin' it,' Douglas said after a long period when only the munching of stale food and the sounds of the horses' progress disturbed the stillness. 'He didn't mean no harm.'

'He just happened to be in the wrong place at the wrong time,' Hedges replied flatly.

'He was railroaded,' Forrest growled.

Hedges heeled his horse into a faster pace and the Union men in Confederate grey were swallowed up by the safe darkness of the Georgia night.

*   *   *

'You will be kind enough to remain still like the rock.'

Edge snapped open his eyes and looked out from under his hat brim at the smooth face of the Chinese sitting opposite him. Then he lowered his gaze and his eyes became mere lines of iced blue as he

52

saw the twin muzzles of the sawn-off double-barrelled shotgun.

'And I thought you guys only ran restaurants,' he muttered.

'Life is full of little surprises,' the Chinese replied.

Edge shifted his gaze and saw that the man diagonally across from him and the one seated beside him were drawing their hands apart and taking out sawn-off shot-guns of their own from the capacious sleeves of their robes.

'My God, a gun!' a woman at the centre of the swaying car screamed.

'Everyone keep calm, no one get hurt,' a Chinese announced in loud tones. He was at the front of the car and rose, turning to look down the aisle and the passengers on either side. His face was as devoid of expression as those of his colleagues. 'We take money and valuables. Not wish take life.'

Alvin and Beth looked fearfully at each other. The boy clutched the woman's hand in his and it was difficult to tell whether he was offering comfort or seeking it. He shot a glance over his shoulder, finding the gaze of Edge and receiving no consolation from the hooded eyes.

'You will please allow my men to relieve you of your arms,' the leader of the Chinese demanded flatly. He pitched his voice just loud enough to be heard above the clatter of the train as the locomotive hauled its burden through the mountains on the California-Nevada state line.

The shotgun maintained an unwavering aim at Edge's stomach and the tall half-breed offered no resistance as the man beside him slid the revolver

53

from his holster and picked up the Winchester from where it rested. Throughout the car, most of the men complied in a similar manner as the carefully positioned Chinese menaced them with shot-guns. But one man, sitting two seats ahead of Edge on the other side of the aisle, snarled a protest. He wore a business suit and no gunbelt. But a bulge beneath his jacket revealed the presence of a small pistol in a shoulder holster. He was fast on the draw, but not fast enough.

'Mao!' a Chinese voice called.

The leader still had his hands clasped together across his middle, concealed by the drape of the robe's sleeves. But now he snapped them apart and he held a pair of short bladed knives decorated with brass and tortoise-shell. One of them *zinged* away from him with a mere flick of a wrist. The blade flashed in the sunlight and sank into the throat of the man who was not fast enough. He made a gurgling sound and his ornate Parkhouse pepperbox clattered to the floor. He toppled sideways on to the gun, his severed jugular vein spraying an arc of blood.

'Not wish to, but will,' Mao announced easily, his voice cutting through the gasps of shocked women.

A bandit reached down and jerked the knife from the throat of the dead man. It came free with an obscene sucking sound. He grinned as he wiped the blade against the dress of a middle-aged woman who was petrified by terror.

'White dress not suit you,' he said. 'Red colour make it pretty.'

'Mr. Shin will now pass among you,' Mao an-

54

nounced calmly. 'You put money and valuables in sack. Very angry if more trouble. Any man attempts to make it, he dies. So does woman—any woman I choose.'

As he spoke, Mao's almond-shaped eyes moved often to linger upon Beth, finding particular interest in the swelling flesh of her breasts revealed by the low neckline of her gown. Alvin was aware of this and a mixture of anger and fear caused his hand to tremble upon that of the woman. But she remained calm, exuding a kind of feminine arrogance as she was forced to submit to the Chinese's probing gaze.

The bandits had been well drilled for the hold-up. Their actions were calm and unhurried as they rose and padded in equal numbers to each end of the car, the aim of the shotguns steady despite the additional burden of the confiscated weapons. Then one of them rested his gun and took out a burlap sack from beneath his robe. He started from the front of the car and moved down the aisle, holding the sack open in front of each passenger. Money, watches, jewellery and a varied selection of gold and silver articles dropped into the sack. While this was in progress, one Chinese at each end of the car opened a window and tossed out the passengers' guns.

Edge had seven and a half thousand dollars split into small bundles and tucked inside his shirt. As he unbuttoned the shirt and reached inside, bringing out the bundles one at a time, Shin's eyes grew wider and wider.

'You very rich man,' the Chinese said as Edge held out his hands, palms upward to indicate there was no more.

'Easy come, easy go,' the half-breed said softly.

'You no have to work for money?'

'Killing people ain't work,' Edge replied.*

'That what Mr Mao think,' Shin said with a hint of pride.

'A man of deep thought,' Edge said.

When Shin had completed his task, one gun-toting Chinese was left at each end of the car while the remainder moved to the cars ahead and behind. The passengers remained silent, many having to struggle within themselves to keep from looking at the slumped form of the dead man.

Edge looked idly out of the window as the locomotive slowed and strained to haul the cars up a steep gradient which was one of the steps across the Sierras. The sun was still bright, but the mountain air had grown chill and in the far distance, across a vista of verdant pine forests and jagged, barren rock crests, snow could be seen frosting the highest peaks.

At the front of the car, Alvin and Beth continued to hold hands. The woman's sensual features were devoid of expression, reflecting a mind prepared to accept and deal with each problem as it arose. Her ill-matched partner was pale faced and tense of posture as he struggled against an involuntary impulse to explode his frustration. And he was able to contain his emotions by forcing his mind to accept the hold-up as poetic justice. He had stolen two thousand dollars from his father to finance the elopement with Beth. Now it had been stolen from

*See: *Edge: Blood on Silver* and *Edge: California Killing.*

56

him. He could but hope that her love for him was strong enough to stand the test of poverty.

The train reached the top of the grade and picked up speed again as it thrust into a steep-sided ravine, parallel with the course of a swiftly running stream. The two gunshots echoed along the ravine, crystal clear against the clatter of the train, which immediately began to slow with a screeching of brakes.

'Sound like train men make trouble for Mr Mao,' the Chinese at the rear of the car said.

'Should have listened to your head man's warning,' Edge responded with a sigh.

The Chinese allowed a smile to alter the impassiveness of his smooth features. 'Sometimes Mr Mao forget to speak American. Talk to people in Mandarin.'

'Orange Chinese for Christ's sake,' Edge muttered.

'How disgustingly inhuman!' the woman with the blood-stained dress exclaimed shrilly.

The Chinese shook his head. 'Mr Mao think all people of world should speak his language.'

'Very unpolitic,' Edge muttered.

Chapter Four

THEY rode hard through the hours of darkness, and whenever Captain Hedges called a halt he was thinking more of conserving the strength of the horses rather than rest for the men. Safely attired in their Confederate uniforms they kept to the main trails and turnpikes, heading north by the stars glimmering intermittently through the storm clouds. Those civilians who happened to see the group of seven riders cantering through the night seldom spared them a second glance. There was a war on and the sight of soldiery in a hurry was a common one.

Thus, Hedges and his men did not deviate to avoid the hamlets, villages and small towns which straddled their route. And as the hour grew late there was even less risk of being challenged for the men were riding through a farming belt and the people who lived there retired early in preparation for a new day.

When the eastern horizon began to pale with the first streaks of greyness marking the false dawn they were riding along a narrow turnpike which ran as straight as an arrow across open countryside towards a vast expanse of pine wood.

Hedges, his own pallor wan beneath the dark brown of its natural pigmentation, turned in the saddle to survey the faces of the men strung out behind him. He saw fatigue and hunger etched in their every line, strong enough to almost cancel out the set of cruelty and lurking hatred which war and imprisonment had sculptored against their flesh. The pace he had set through the night had drained them of the meagre energy they had stored from the sleep at the farm and pitifully small amount of food they had stolen from the dead Rebel's saddlebags.

Forrest, riding immediately behind the captain, sensed the stare from the hooded eyes and dragged his chin up off his chest.

'You want something, Captain?' he rasped.

It had been the first time in many miles since anybody had spoken and the other troopers dragged their attention to the head of the column.

'Yeah,' Hedges answered. 'Soon as we get in the trees up ahead, we'll rest.'

'Thank God for that,' Rhett muttered.

'You're a great guy for camp, ain't you, Bob?' Bell answered and managed a hollow guffaw.

They continued on down the turnpike in silence and when it plunged into the trees Hedges kept to the road for over a hundred yards before he angled away, trampling the thickly growing undergrowth until the ground opened out into a grassy dell. As the men followed his example by sliding from their saddles, Seward and Douglas began to unsaddle their horses.

'Forget it,' Hedges snapped, unhooking his canteen and drawing the razor from its neck pouch. 'We ain't staying.'

60

'Aw, Captain,' Seward whined.

Forrest looked at Hedges with questioning aggression. 'We ain't goin' to make the Union lines in one hop, Captain,' he said softly.

'We ain't going to make them at all if we ride through the south looking like hobos,' Hedges answered as he unscrewed the stopper from the canteen and splashed water on his face. 'Highest rank we can muster is sergeant. We run into a Johnnie Reb officer he ain't so likely to ask questions if we look like soldiers.'

He squatted down with his back against a tree trunk and began to rasp the finely honed blade of the razor through the thick growing black bristles. Without soap to lubricate the skin, each stroke of the razor sounded like a renting of stout cloth and some of the men winced.

Forrest took the razor hurriedly when Hedges had finished and was using more water to wash dried sweat and grime from his face.

'You seem mighty anxious to inflict that torture on yourself,' Steward said.

As Forrest began to slice through his own bristles, he grinned at the grimacing youngster. 'We only got the one blade, Billy,' he pointed out. 'And we ain't got no strop.'

Rhett swallowed hard. 'I think I'll grow a beard,' he muttered.

'You'll shave!' Hedges said with low venom, as he dusted off his uniform with the flat of his hand. 'Or you'll get shaved—and I won't stop short at the hair on your face.'

61

'He ain't got none anyplace else, Captain,' Douglas put in.

'How'd you get to find that out, Hal?' Bell taunted.

'Guess the fairies must have told him,' Scott returned.

'Cut out the yakking!' Forrest snarled. He tossed the razor to Seward. 'And do like the Captain says. Or there won't be one of you with even an eyelash left.'

The men fell silent, waiting their turn to use the razor and afterwards doing what they could to clean themselves and their uniforms.

'What's the plan, Captain?' Forrest asked at length.

Hedges clicked his tongue against the back of his teeth and watched the disgruntled troopers as they performed their ablutions. 'Atlanta's up ahead.' He replied without looking at the mean-faced sergeant. 'I figure the turnpike goes straight into the city. That ain't for us. Place will be crawling with Rebels and we don't want any awkward questions to answer. So we gotta look for a town with food and beds. One without any other uniforms in it. After we've rested we'll swing around the city and keep heading north 'till we hear shooting.'

Forrest pondered this, then nodded. 'Guess I can't think of nothing beter than that,' he allowed.

Hedges met and held his flinty gaze. 'I figured that,' the Captain replied and turned to examine the men.

The comparative cleanness of their faces served to emphasise the emaciating effects of deprivation and malnutrition and he knew it would take time rather than water and a blade to rid their eyes of the haunted look. Perhaps, he considered, the men would never shed it until death blotted out their memories. He spat into the grass.

'Sure don't look like any West Point class of 'sixty-three,' he pronounced. 'Let's move out.'

The true dawn had broken now and as they returned to the road and the trees began to thin out, the lightening of the new day was accompanied by a noticeable warming of the air. On the far side of the wood the country was undulating and the turnpike began to curve to left and right, swinging around and between the hills, taking the easiest course. They had ridden perhaps two miles from the wood when they saw the village, nestling under the brow of a hill amid a patchwork of tobacco fields.

It was comprised of just a few houses, dominated by a church, and looked deserted in the sudden brightness from a sun tightening its hold on the eastern horizon. Hedges led the troopers through the refreshing coolness of a stream forded by the turnpike and then angled off on to a spur which followed the course of the water run up to the village.

The village was spread along one bank of the stream, on both sides of a short street which dead ended at the church. From below, the setting had looked almost idyllic, but up close the impression was suddenly altered. The houses, two drying barns, saloon and general store all looked on the verge of collapse. But, strangely at odds with the warped and unpainted dereliction of the timber buildings there was a neat orderliness in evidence. Sagging sidewalks were swept clean of dust; those windows

63

which were not broken shone with recent polishing; curtains, although patched and darned, were as white as the day they were bought; and the church at the end of the street might have been built yesterday, so well had it been kept.

As Hedges halted in the centre of the street before the church and the troopers reined in their own mounts, an eerie silence descended upon the sunlit scene, broken only by the gentle babbling from the stream. Several hands strayed towards rifle stocks or revolver butts as the highly-developed sixth sense of each man warned him not to trust the stillness.

'I don't like it,' Forrest said in a whisper. But the deceptive somnolence magnified the words.

'Even less if you draw one of them weapons,' a woman's voice snapped.

Several doors creaked on unoiled hinges and the men moved their hands slowly, looking up and down each side of the street.

'Will you look at that,' Seward rasped, the breath whistling out of him as his mouth took on the line of a leering smile.

There were thirteen of them and only one did not have a rifle levelled at the knot of riders. The exception was an aged pastor who stood in the arched doorway of the church. The rest were women, stretching across an age span of early-twenties to late sixties. All were dressed to a pattern in modest, well-cared for black gowns topped by crisp white aprons. Each guarded a doorway, her face set in a hard expression which left no doubt she was prepared to use the ancient single-shot muzzle-loader she held so firmly.

'You've looked,' a stout, middle-aged redhead in the entrance to the small saloon barked. 'Now turn around and get out of town.'

She motioned with the gun.

'We need food and shelter to rest up,' Hedges said evenly.

'You won't find it here,' the spokeswoman replied harshly.

The Captain saw there would be no relenting on her part, so turned his attention to the minister. 'That so, reverend?' he asked.

The man was in his eighties, thin and stooped, with withered features and sparse silver hair worn in a well-trimmed fringe. His voice was as weak as his appearance. 'I am here to care for the souls of these women, my son,' he said. 'Since all their menfolk were killed in the war they have only their belief to sustain them. I confine myself to nurturing their faith in the Almighty. In all other respects they are self-sufficient and I do not interfere.'

'You understand that, soldier boy?' the redhead demanded. 'He means that what we say goes. And we say go.'

The woman commanded only the attention of Hedges. The rest of the men were looking at the younger, prettier widows. And a few of the women were responding to the inquisitive scrutiny by softening the lines of their expressions.

'We're about beat, ma'am,' Hedges said at length. 'And I reckon there ain't nothing we wouldn't do for some food and some sleep. So I guess we'll have to take the risk you widows will blast us and make seven more of your own kind.'

65

This captured the attention of the troopers and they watched fearfully as the Captain dismounted. His movements were cautious but determined and all the time the slits of his eyes kept a steady watch on the woman.

'You don't look like no married men,' she challenged.

'Long time from the well,' Hedges replied, motioning for the men to slide from their saddles. He grinned with his mouth.

'You ain't going to slake your thirst here,' the redhead retaliated. Her aggressive attitude did not alter: but neither did she offer any further threat as the troopers dismounted.

Hedges nodded his agreement. His cold grin faded and his lean features showed menace as he raked his eyes across the faces of the men. 'Any of you try to use your dipper in this town, he'll answer to me.'

A hot, empty silence gripped the street again. The redheaded woman broke it with a single word.

'Padre?'

The old man was sweating. He allowed the tension to drain out of him on a long sigh. 'They will not be swayed,' he said tremulously. 'You must either trust them or kill them. I am pleased the decision is not mine to make.'

The woman pondered while the men waited. Finally she stepped back into the shadowed doorway of her house and when she re-emerged she no longer held the gun.

'Thou shalt not kill!' she exclaimed.

'There are nine more of those,' Hedges hissed to the suddenly smiling men as the rest of the women

66

laid down their arms. 'You break any of them in this town, I'll break you—in little pieces.'

'Christ, Captain!' Seward murmured as the women moved out into the street, towards the men.

'Higher than Him,' Hedges hissed into the lustful face of the youngster. 'I'm an officer and you're an enlisted man. That makes me God.'

'I am Gilda Proctor, sergeant,' the red-head introduced herself, and proceeded to point to each of the women in turn, announcing their names, 'Maria Marwick, Vivien Bull, Faith Terry . . .'

Hedges did not hear the other names because he was no longer listening. And when he failed to reciprocate and Rhett's good breeding came to the fore and the New Englander named the men, the half-breed continued to study the thirty-year-old blonde woman called Faith Terry. She was large breasted and thick of hips and her face, which had once been pretty was now aged beyond its years by the harshness of life. She responded to his scrutiny with an initial nervousness which quickly became close to guarded invitation as she misinterpreted his source of interest.

Terry was a name that raised a low fire of hatred in his heart.

Other women looked at individual troopers with a similar degree of feminine wiliness, but there was no mistaking the men's innermost thoughts.

'You will please go to the church,' Gilda instructed. 'Food will be brought to you there. We will then discuss sleeping arrangements.'

Her words and the discontented murmuring of the troopers brought Hedges' mind back from out of the past. 'We'll do like the lady says,' he ordered. Then he reached up and slid the Spencer from his saddle boot. 'Against regulations to let these out of our sight.'

It angered the red-head, but Hedges' steady stare forced a nod of approval from her. The troopers withdrew their own rifles.

'We'll take care of your horses,' Faith Terry assured Hedges, who nodded and followed the men through the arched entrance into the murky coolness of the church. There was not a speck of dust to be seen anywhere and the wooden pews, stone altar and silver effigies showed the reward of loving care.

The minister was kneeling before the altar and rose painfully to his feet as the men slouched down on to the pews. 'I have prayed that you will honour your word,' the old man said thinly. He grimaced as Forrest rolled a cigarette and lit it, striking a match against the polished pew. 'Even if you have no faith in God and respect for His house.'

'They're beyond redemption, padre,' Hedges said, reaching across to pluck the cigarette from Forrest's fingers.

The sergeant started to snarl, but it became a grin as he saw Hedges draw deeply against the cigarette. He began to roll another.

'How about the word of the women?' Hedges asked. 'Can we trust that?'

'In what way, my son?'

'That they're all widows?'

The minister's thin shoulders moved in a shrug.

'Most know for sure. The rest have been so long without word from their men, they have been forced to abandon hope.'

'How about Faith—?'

'They have that in the Lord.'

Hedges shook his head. 'Faith Terry, Padre.'

The minister's mournful face became set in an even more melancholy line. 'She cannot expect to hear officially. Her husband was always something of a renegade. He chose to evade regular army service and formed a guerilla band.'

'Hey, Cap . . . !' Seward exclaimed, then shrilled his pain as Forrest's boot cracked into his ankle.

'Yeah, Billy,' Hedges muttered, grinding out his cigarette under his heel. 'We all remember Bill Terry.'

The minister's expression brightened and the light of hope flared in his eyes. 'You've seen him recently?'

'It seems like only yesterday,' Hedges replied softly, rising from the pew and moving back to the doorway where he stood, staring out along the sun-bright street and across the well-tended tobacco fields.

There was activity in the town now. Down at the bank of the stream three of the women were watering the horses, having already removed the saddles. Smoke curling up into the still air from several chimneys, and a mouth-watering smell of frying bacon and beans evidenced the task allocated to the other women. The scrape of boot leather on the stone floor drew Hedges' attention to Forrest, who had come to stand beside him.

'Terry killed your girl, Captain,' the mean-faced
69

sergeant said softly. 'And because you went after him, we got captured and shipped to Andersonville.'

'So?' Hedges answered, his gaze meeting and holding the steely eyes of the other man.

'The boys ain't gonna take kindly to risking their lives to settle your scores.'

Hedges stabbed a finger at the chevrons on his arm. 'We're in a different army now,' he hissed. 'I been demoted but I still outrank you. Bell's got chevrons. I ain't asking no favours.'

Forrest sent a length of spit splatting into the dust outside. 'Terry could be dead—or a thousand miles from here.'

Hedges looked back at the street as six women appeared from as many houses, carrying trays upon which food and coffee steamed invitingly. 'I feel lucky,' he said softly.

One of the women was Faith Terry and she was again responsive to the Captain's staring eyes as she moved into the church with the other women. As the minister bowed to the altar, begging forgiveness for the sacrilege, the troopers roared their approval of the food and at once began to wolf it down.

The women watched, some with disgust, others with pity, as the men ate. The meal was over when the grimfaced Gilda entered the church.

'The three houses at the end of the street have been vacated for you, sergeant,' she told Hedges. 'There are enough beds for all of you. We would ask you to go to the houses and not come out until you are ready to leave town. Which we hope will be soon.'

'It's a deal,' Hedges agreed, and once again the

70

raking of his hooded eyes over the faces of the men was enough to stem voicing of their discontent. And as he rose and moved out into the street, the troopers followed him. Now that their hunger had been appeased, a stronger need was kindled in their stomachs, over-riding fatigue. Lust was like a heavy burden, dragging their feet to stir up dust as they ambled along the street. Rhett, alone, was at ease.

'You ain't gonna be able to hold 'em much longer,' Forrest whispered to Hedges. 'It's been a long time since the last time. I figure they're ready to kill for a piece of ass—anybody.'

'They'll have to,' Hedges replied evenly. 'How many horses do you see down by the stream, Forrest?'

The sergeant looked in the direction the Captain indicated and his mouth formed into a thin line. 'Six is one less than there ought to be,' he muttered, and his head swivelled, his mouth moving soundlessly as he did a head count of the women. 'The Marwick dame ain't around no more.'

They were almost at the designated houses now and could speak at normal pitch without being overheard by their reluctant hosts.

'Reckon they went back on their word,' Hedges said. 'Won't feel so bad about breaking mine.'

'The word of God is in my language for a change!' Seward exclaimed in delight.

Hedges opened the door of one of the broken down houses and halted, turning to face the exalted men. 'Get some rest,' he instructed.

'Ain't rest we want some of, Captain,' Seward whined.

Hedges, lips curled back to show his teeth in a harsh grin. 'You need to sleep,' he said. 'Go off half-cocked and likely you won't rise to the occasion.'

'He's got a point, Billy,' Forrest said.

'So have I,' Seward answered dully.

'We can all see,' Rhett put in, leering. 'It's sticking out like a sore thumb.'

'That's about the size of it,' Forrest responded, and guffawed as he headed for the door of the house next door.

Down the street the women watched in silence as the Union troopers in Rebel grey entered the houses and closed the doors. Then the old man came out of the church.

'Do you think we fooled them, Mrs Proctor?' he asked nervously.

The grim-faced red-head drew in a deep breath and expelled it as a sigh. 'We've done our best, reverend,' she replied. 'But I'll feel a whole lot safer when Terry's Raiders get here.'

*   *   *

'You, you and you!' Shin said as he re-entered the car and stabbed a well-manicured finger at Alvin, Beth and Edge.

'What?' the boy asked nervously.

'Mr Mao wishes to dissuade pursuit,' the Chinese replied. 'So we take three hostages from each car. All hostages die if we followed.'

An old lady with silver hair and a kindly face gasped. 'Surely you cannot be so cruel?' she accused.

Mr. Shin smiled. 'We no cruel. No suffering. Kill quick.'

The shotgun swung up and both barrels belched smoke. Many passengers covered their ears against the roar of the explosion which was almost painful within the confines of the car. The old lady no longer had a kind face. She was thrown back against her seat, then toppled forward on to the floor, the gaping, blood-spurting holes in her flesh tinged black by the powder of the short-range shot.

'She feel no pain,' Mr Shin announced, still smiling. In the sudden silence, he cocked his head on one side, listening. A series of shotgun blasts rippled down the length of the halted train and he nodded. 'Picture worth a thousand words,' he said to the horrified passengers. 'Now everyone have no doubt we mean business.'

He barked a command in Chinese and the two guards moved away from their positions, one aiming his shotgun at Alvin and Beth, the other covering Edge.

'You come now!' Shin commanded.

Alvin and Beth looked over their shoulders towards Edge. The half-breed got slowly to his feet and ambled along the aisle, stepping over the dead man and glancing down at the mutilated face of the old lady. Her hair was no longer silver as it floated in a wide pool of her own blood.

'The money fell their way,' he muttered. 'Heads, they win.'

The second guard made a threatening motion with his shotgun and Alvin scrambled to his feet, urging the woman to rise beside him.

The hostages were hustled out on to the car's platform and then down on to the grassy bank of

73

the stream. A dozen prisoners—nine men and three women—were already there, herded into a frightened group. Other members of the gang had been spread throughout the train for there were now a score of robed Chinese surrounding the group, staring at the hostages from the deep shadows cast by their coolie hats. Four of them had the sacks of loot slung over their shoulders. The remainder, with the exception of Mao, cradled shotguns. The leader had his hands clasped under the veil of his sleeves. Shin conferred with him and Mao rapped out an order.

Edge glanced around at his fellow prisoners and saw the near paralysing fear lurking in eyes that still mirrored the bloody slaughter they had witnessed.

'Mr Mao say form two lines,' Shin instructed. 'We march to camp.'

The hostages shuffled into the formation required. Edge was at the end of the line, next to a trembling, middle-aged drummer whose face was sheened with sweat dried by the chill mountain air. Alvin and Beth were in front of him.

Shin nodded in smiling approval and suddenly pointed at the two men heading the line. 'You. Face each other. Hold hands.'

The two did as ordered and Mao approached them, inclined his head and turned his back to them.

'You carry Mr Mao across the water,' Shin ordered and the two men crouched. Mao sat upon their clasped hands and was lifted clear of the ground. The smooth-faced gang leader rattled out a rapid stream of Chinese and Shin pumped his head in

74

acknowledgement. 'We go now. Mr Mao say, you drop him you regret day mothers tell fathers okay. Okay?'

The two men nodded emphatically and as Shin smiled in approval, they moved forward, splashing ankle deep into the icy coldness of the rushing stream. Flanked by the guards, the line of hostages followed. The passengers left on the train stared from the windows with wide-eyed concern as the prisoners and their captives waded through the sparkling water, the men at the front being forced to raise their burden higher and higher as the level of the water rose almost to waist level at the mid-way point.

The quaking fear of most of the hostages was supplemented by shivering cold as they climbed up on to the opposite bank.

Mao rattled out a further order and Shin smiled at the two men heading the line. 'Mr Mao thanks you.'

They lowered their burden with sighs of relief, flexing their aching muscles. Mao whispered to Shin, who looked along the line, nodded, then strode towards the end. He halted beside Alvin and Beth. His smiling eyes lingered on the woman's cleavage.

'Mr Mao asks that the lady walk beside him.'

Beth's sensuous features showed nothing of what she thought about the request. But anger broke through Alvin's fear and his complexion darkened to a purple hue. He tightened his grip on the woman's hand.

'No!' he rasped, and his eyes pleaded with her. 'Beth?'

She managed to force a smile for him. 'If it'll keep us alive, dear,' she said softly.

Alvin hesitated, fear fighting fury behind his young face. Suddenly every shotgun was pointed at him.

'Mr Mao no like to be kept waiting,' Shin urged.

Tension stretched like an invisible band around the group, threatening to snap with an explosion of sudden death. Edge's words were like an escape valve.

'She figures she can handle him.'

Alvin read the implication behind the remark and spun around, seeking to vent his frustration on a man apparently as helpless as himself. But as his blazing eyes became locked on Edge's ice cold stare he saw an enormous latent power and became hypnotised into immobility. Beth jerked free of his grip and stepped out of the line.

'I'll keep the guy company,' she said to Shin, the tone and her expression revealing the well-learned lessons of her former profession.

'That good,' Shin replied, motioning with his empty shotgun.

Her deportment was also a carefully calculated ploy and despite the danger of their situation, few of the male hostages could quell a stab of desire as they watched the woman's swaying hips and thrusting breasts. When she halted alongside Mao, she smiled beguilingly at him and he bowed slightly from the waist.

The line moved forward again, angling away from the stream and the railroad, towards a cleft in the side of the ravine. And they had not gone many

yards before Mao unfolded his arms and laid a proprietary hand on Beth's vibrant rump, the yellow
fingers splaying before forming into a lustful claw.

Alvin snarled, his head bobbing to and fro as he
peered ahead along the line of marching prisoners.

'You just got to admit it, Alvin,' Edge muttered
to the boy. 'Mao can't lose any way it falls. He won
it with the head. Now he's got the tail.'

Chapter Five

THE troopers used only two of the houses offered them, and neither of these for sleeping. Rhett, Bell and Douglas joined Hedges; and Seward and Scott followed Forrest into the house next door. They were little more than cabins, single storeyed with a sparsely furnished sitting room and a bedroom and kitchen each. In common with their outward appearance, they were neatly kept and extremely clean, but loose hinges, warped boards and sagging shelves witnessed the long absence of men to attend to such chores.

'What the hell's happening?' Bell wanted to know as the Captain assigned his section of the troop to keep watch from the windows.

Hedges peered out through a cracked pane at the street. 'You know the facts of life, trooper?' he hissed.

'Aw, come on, Captain,' Bell answered. 'You let me out with those dames and I'll show you.'

'So how come there's that many women in this town and no kids around?'

Douglas was guarding the kitchen window at the rear. 'Hey, I never thought of that!' he exclaimed.

Hedges grinned mirthlessly out at the empty street as he heard the church door slam shut. Then a bolt was shot home. 'That's because when you men got screwing on your minds, you can't think.'

Rhett was in the bedroom. His nervousness could be heard in his voice. 'And if they really trusted us, they'd be no reason to keep the children hidden?'

'Smart,' Hedges complimented with heavy sarcasm. 'And if you could count as well you'd know that one of our horses and one of the women have gone.'

'Man!' Bell breathed.

'I figure more than one,' Hedges responded in low tones.

'Why, Captain?' Rhett called anxiously from the bedroom. 'I can't figure any of this. Georgia's Rebel land. You reckon those women realised we're Union?'

'I ain't doing anymore figuring until I see who the missing woman brings back with her,' Hedges answered. 'Now cut out the yakking. We're supposed to be sleeping.'

Bell swallowed hard, his eyes swivelling up and down the street, narrowing against the glare of sunlight, coming wide to peer into the deep shadows thrown by buildings.

'Suddenly I ain't tired,' he whispered to himself.

For an hour nothing moved in the tiny town and the sole noise came from the stream in its ceaseless rush to tumble down to the foot of the rise. Then the seven troopers heard a sound invade the silence from far off: and as it grew steadily in volume they were able to pin down the direction. It was coming from the north-west. And moments later, just before it came to an abrupt end, they identified it. A group of horsemen riding at the gallop.

In the last house but one on the street, Frank Forrest bared his crooked, tobacco-stained teeth in an evil grin. 'Figure to creep up on us, Billy,' he said softly.

Seward nodded and checked the action of his Spencer. 'How many you reckon, Frank?'

'Sure ain't no regiment,' the sergeant answered. 'Don't figure they'll give us much trouble.'

Forrest was at one of the front windows of the house, Seward at the other. Scott crouched in the bedroom. Each man had been fighting drowsiness in the heat and silence of the waiting: but now they were alert, keyed up for action—even exhilarated by the prospect of renewed killing.

A similar pulse of excited anticipation throbbed in the hearts of the eleven men advancing up the slope on the town side of the stream, from where their horses were held by the woman who summoned them. Their ages spanned a broad spectrum, from very young to past sixty, their builds from short and rotund to tall and emaciated and their garb from dishevelled Confederate uniforms to ill-used denim. But despite the obvious differences between them, there was a certain uniformity about the men which could be identified in the set of their grizzled faces and the haunted, deep-set eyes. For here could be seen the look of the hunted, cowering behind the thin veneer of triumph as the fugitive sensed a much sought reversal.

And as the men drew nearer their objective, the desire for revenge showed most vividly in the dark,

81

red-veined eyes of their leader, Bill Terry. For it was in him that the seeds of bitterness had been sewn deepest. He was a short, compactly built man of forty-one who had served his apprenticeship in the art of cruelty as slavemaster on a Virginia cotton plantation before becoming a bank robber. Then had come the Civil War and he had elected to evade regular army service in the Confederate cause and chosen to fight a guerilla campaign. The band of stage robbers, rapists, con men and murderers who followed him took his orders not because of his self-appointment to the rank of captain, but because he proved himself to be the meanest and toughest man in the group, particularly in using a sabre captured from a union officer.

It had been a good war for him, until his raiders hit the Union camp at Murfreesboro in the summer of sixty-two and abducted some women. A troop of Union cavalry had given chase and of the raiders, Terry was the sole survivor, making good his escape after burning an officer's lady at the stake.

Since then, his war had turned sour and he could no longer wage a hit-and-run campaign against the North with the support of the Richmond administration. For word of his atrocity had been communicated to the Confederate capital and both the army and civil authorities had issued "wanted" posters on him. Thus, he was forced to adopt the tactics of his pre-war days as a criminal—stealing, running and hiding in company with the human dregs who comprised his newly formed raiders.

But now, as the distance between the group and the town narrowed, Terry could almost taste vengeance. Up ahead, sleeping in their innocence of impending slaughter, was a unit of Confederate cavalry. And Terry had no doubt that it was one of many such units scouring Georgia for him, following a successful bank raid in Atlanta. It was their ill-luck—and his good fortune—that found them sleeping off their exhaustion trapped in a town which he had claimed as home for the raiders' wives and families.

At the top of the rise, where the spur of the trail levelled out to feed the town's single street, Terry raised a hand, halting the men. Then he motioned with his other hand, which clutched the hilt of his sabre, instructing the men to split into two groups. One group, led by Terry, continued on up the street while the second angled towards the rear of the houses.

'Hey,' Seward whispered as he drew a bead on one of the raiders. 'Ain't that . . . ?'

'That's him,' Forrest cut in. 'The Captain was right about his luck. Don't break it for him.'

'What?'

'Don't reckon he'll take kindly to anybody else killing Terry.'

From the outside, there was nothing about the houses to arouse the suspicion of the raiders as they crept forward, for sunlight bouncing against the window panes at the front acted as an opaque screen for the men behind them. And at the rear, Scott, Douglas and Rhett stayed low or to the side.

The raiders first surrounded the house at the end of the street, moving with silent caution. From the church, the women watched with bated breath, aware that the house was empty but knowing a shout of warning could also alert the soldiers.

As he neared the front door, Terry drew a Colt from his holster and nodded to two men to cover the window with their rifles. Then he gave a low whistle and the men at the rear closed in. Terry, his grizzled face twisted into a mask of hatred, raised a foot and sent his boot crashing into the door. As it slammed wide, he rushed inside, and two windows smashed in the rear.

'They ain't here!' he roared and the men ringing the house whirled, fear crawling across their faces.

For long moments the familiar silence gripped the town and the sole movements were the swivelling of the raiders' eyes as they sought to explore every hiding place. Then Terry exploded an animalistic bellow of frustration and his boot thudded against floorboards as he ran to the door.

'Blast 'em!' Hedges yelled.

Seven rifles cracked with a sound like a single cannon shot. Four raiders screamed and reeled drunkenly before slumping to the ground, pumping blood from head and chest wounds. Two survivors on the street turned and scuttled for the cover of the houses opposite. One of them reached safety but the second was launched into a clumsy cartwheeling motion as a bullet from Forrest's rifle took the man high in the thigh. He dropped his gun and tried to drag himself one-handed across the sun-baked street as his other hand clawed at the blood-soaked raggedness of his jeans. The rest of the raiders ran into the house where Terry stood, trembling in a rage, shrieking a string of obscenities.

'Come on, Cookie!' the raider on the far side of the street yelled, not daring to break cover to help the injured man.

'Yeah, Cookie!' Seward taunted. 'Get the lead outta your pants!'

'For Christ's sake, they'll kill you!'

The injured man clawed at the hard ground, his features painted with agony. His body snaked forward a pitiful few inches. Four shots rang out simultaneously and pieces of bloodied flesh and shiny bone splinters spun away from the back of the man's head. His face snapped forward into the ground and he lay still.

'Bastards!' the man across the street screamed.

'Just the way the Cookie crumbles!' Forrest taunted in reply.

Since the houses were built in a straight line neither group could see its enemy and only the man who had reached the other side of the street was in a position to assess the situation.

'Hemingway!' Terry yelled.

'Yeah, Bill?' The man's voice was still shaky with shock.

'What d'you see?'

'House next door and the one next to that.'

Terry, sweating, irritatingly aware of the five pairs of eyes looking to him for a decision, began to pace the room.

'We got took, Bill,' a bearded fifty-year-old complained. 'Them army guys must have smelled a rat.'

Terry's arm swung and the sabre point was suddenly resting against the man's middle. 'Must have been you,' Terry snarled. 'You stink of fear.'

85

The man's beard quivered. 'Yeah, Bill,' he agreed. 'But what we gonna do?'

Terry snorted, spun away from the man and went to the window. He stared out at the empty street. 'We're gonna wait, that's what,' he hissed. 'We're gonna sweat the army into making first move.'

And the troopers were sweating. The air inside the houses was cloyed with stale heat and the tension of knowing that sudden death lurked only feet away was a strong additional factor in sheening the men's faces with moisture.

'Reckon they're waiting for us to do somethin', Captain?' Bell whispered.

Hedges finished reloading his Spencer and pumped a shell into the breech. 'They sure as hell ain't taking a coffee break,' he answered.

'So what we gonna do?' Bell asked.

'Keep 'em from getting bored,' Hedges replied, stepping to the door and jerking it open.

Hemingway, one of the few raiders wearing a semblance of army uniform—a forage cap—heard the creak of the door. He poked his rifle around the corner of the house and fired one blind shot. His bullet had not found a wild mark in the roof before the Spencers of Bell and Hedges spat lead. Wood splinters flew into the raider's face, hard and jagged enough to draw blood. As he screamed and threw up his hands to his face, his rifle clattered down on to the street.

'Farewell to an arm,' Hedges muttered as Forrest and Seward sent a volley of bullets towards Hemingway's position, driving the man further back from the corner.

86

In the vibrant silence that followed the burst of gunfire the heat seemed to increase in intensity. But then the sound of running feet caused every man in the three houses to tighten his grip on his rifle. But the footfalls were moving away from the street and Hedges grinned as he spotted the retreating figure of Hemingway.

Terry bellowed his rage and the shot that was sent after the fleeing man came from his gun. It dug up dirt short of the target and Hemingway splashed through the stream and scuttled towards a stand of trees halfway down the slope.

'The bastard ran out on us!' Terry roared.

'He ain't ready to die,' Hedges taunted. 'It ain't afternoon yet.'

'Where'd he go, Captain?' Bell wanted to know, scanning the street, fearful of attack from another quarter.

'Forget him,' Hedges answered from the open doorway. 'Across the river and into the trees.' He looked along the street towards the church and saw the big door was still firmly closed. 'Get the others,' he instructed and stepped outside, flattening himself against the front wall.

'Bill, they're coming out!' a woman shrieked from the church.

Bell, Rhett and Douglas came through the doorway sideways and then followed Hedges in a crouched run for the gap between the house they had left and the one occupied by the other three troopers. Terry pushed his revolver out of his doorway and sent a wild shot harmlessly across the front of the houses.

'You out there?' Forrest called.

Hedges kept his voice low. 'I'll cover the front. Make it out the rear.'

He stepped away from the corner and began firing along the street, working the action of the Spencer to the limit of its speed. Then, when the gun was empty, he snatched Rhett's rifle and continued in the same manner.

Inside the house Forrest whirled and broke into a run across the sitting room and into the kitchen. Seward was hard on his heels. The sergeant crashed into the rear door and it was ripped off its hinges. As he and Seward burst into the open they began to pour lead towards the house next door. The startled Scott had to crouch down under their line of fire as he made his escape. Only one wild shot was exploded from the rear of Terry's stronghold before the three troopers ducked into cover to join the other four Union men.

Hedges began to reload both the emptied Spencers as Rhett relieved himself against the house wall.

'He's getting better,' Seward rasped. 'Didn't wet his pants this time.'

Hedges threw the New Englander's rifle to him. 'It's the only goddam weapon he's fired all morning.'

Rhett's expression was twisted by the insult, but the Captain's eyes, narrowed again into menacing slits, warned him against a retort.

'We blasted four and one run off,' Forrest said, reloading his own gun. 'I figure six more to go.'

'You count better by the minute,' Hedges complimented sarcastically, motioning the troopers towards the rear end of the entry between the two houses.

'You're gonna enjoy this, Bob,' Scott said softly. 'We're gonna take 'em from behind.'

'You're not funny!' Rhett spat at him.

'Damn right I ain't,' Scott retorted. 'I'm straight.'

'And you've got a big mouth,' Hedges hissed at him. 'Open it once more and you'll be able to flap it from ear to ear.'

Hedges raised his hand and fingered the bulge of the razor pouch at the back of his neck. Long seconds of silence tightened a grip on the troopers. The low croak of Forrest's voice broke it.

'I ain't for all going in ca one side, Captain.'

Hedges let out pent up breath as a sigh and locked his gaze with that of the sergeant. 'The women owe you any favours?' Forrest looked confused. 'They got their eyes on the street. If so much as an ant moves out there, they'll yell at Terry to blast it.'

Forrest considered this while the others watched him. Finally, his expression conceded the truth of Hedges' statement. But he could not allow it to rest there.

'Waiting in the open ain't no better than time-wasting inside,' he challenged.

'So let's go chase the cruds out of there,' the Captain answered.

He tossed his rifle up onto the flat roof of the house, hooked his fingers over the angle of the roof and wall and hauled himself aloft. It took the startled troopers a moment to assimilate this move and then they, too, followed Hedges' example. Seconds later the seven were snaking across the roof on their bellies, using the rifle stocks for levers. Then seven rifle muzzles angled down over the opposite edge of the roof and exploded into a destructive fusillade against the side wall of the house next door.

Inside the house the raiders yelled in alarm, leaping up from their crouched positions to stare at the wall into which bullets were thudding. But only one man was pushed beyond the limit of panic, crashing out through a rear window to roll over once before regaining his feet and breaking into a run.

A snap shot from Seward caught the man high in the back and pitched him to the ground.

'That wall's too thick!' Terry yelled at the remaining raiders as the troopers' guns rattled empty.

'But getting thinner all the time,' Hedges muttered as he fed fresh shells into the magazine and glanced at the yellow line which the bullets had gouged out along the side of the house.

Again a concentrated volley of shots thudded into the wall, sending more splinters flying. Two found entrance. One burrowed into the floor. The second clashed against Terry's sabre blade and ricocheted into the stomach of the bearded man. He screamed, folded forward and began to writhe on the floor. His gun exploded and sent a bullet smashing into the eye of a terrified youngster. The older man's moans of pain and the metallic scraping of fresh rounds into hot rifles were loud, magnified by the sudden cessation of gunfire. Then the reloading was completed and the man died with a gasp that spewed blood from his gaping mouth.

Terry and his three surviving men backed to the far wall, looking with expectant eyes at the ominous holes across the room. Terry's mouth worked silently for a few moments, then the words came out.

'Okay! You got us. We're coming out.'

The troopers on the roof grinned. Hedges' face was impassive.

'Front door. No rifles. Hands on heads.'

The raiders looked at Terry, and were unable to match his grin as he removed his hat, put his Colt underneath and replaced it. But they dropped their rifles and imitated his actions. When he put his hands on his head and walked to the door, the sabre trailed down his back. At the door he turned sideways on, concealing the weapon from the men on the roof.

The troopers got to their feet and stood in a line, Spencers trained on the four men as they filed into the street.

'Two short,' Forrest warned.

'Two dead,' Terry replied, then did a double take at the roof. The craftiness of his expression abruptly changed into a fusion of anger and hatred. 'They're Union!' he shrieked, bending forward, hurling the sabre in a two-handed throw.

As the sabre was still spinning through the air, all four raiders clawed for the concealed revolvers. They got off four shots as the troopers ducked to avoid the flashing steel.

Hedges spun and dropped his rifle, both hands reaching for the fountain of blood spouting from his left thigh. His knees buckled and rapped against the edge of the roof. Then he pitched off, his head

91

thudding into the sun-hardened ground. There was an instant of mind-twisting pain: then the sun seemed to smash into the world, burning it into a charred black void.

He didn't hear the rifles crack, nor see the four raiders slump backwards pouring blood into the thirsty ground. He was unaware of the troopers leaping down from the roof, two entering the house to check on the dead in there while the other four approached the raiders on the street.

'We got us a live one,' Seward exclaimed, lowering his rifle muzzle against the pulsing throat of Bill Terry.

Forrest decorated his features with an evil grin. 'Captain's goin' to like that.'

Seward looked unsympathetically at Hedges lying face down and unmoving, stretching his full six feet three inches across the ground. 'He looks like he could use some good news, Sarge.'

Forrest seemed to have forgotten Hedges had been hit. Now, his mean face devoid of emotion, he crossed to where Hedges was sprawled and put his boot under the stomach of the unconscious man. He flipped him over on to his back. He saw the dark blood staining Hedges' pants and the purple bruise on his forehead.

'If you hate him that much, Frank, you won't get a better chance to kill him,' Seward challenged.

Forrest spat into the dust close to Hedges' unmoving right hand. The five troopers watched him expectantly.

'Ain't many men I've hated worse than him,' Forrest rasped.

'Nor many you've needed more,' Rhett replied softly.

The truth hit home hard and Forrest whirled. His frustration became transmuted into hate as he stared into the scornful eyes of the New Englander. The tension between the two men stretched time. Forrest snapped it.

'But you I can do without, punk,' he snarled. He raised his Spencer and Rhett began to quake.

'Frank, the church!' Scott barked.

All the men turned to look along the street, across the crumpled forms of the dead raiders, to where the church door had opened. The women began to file out, all in black now, having taken off their white aprons. Each one either held, or led by the hand, a small child. They formed up into a line, with the children in front of them, across the doorway of the church.

'Hal, go get the dame and the horses. Rhett, pick up the Captain. Billy, bring the poor man's Quantrill.'

Forrest's voice was soft, but commanded instant compliance. As the designated men moved to carry out their orders, the church bell sounded: the slow, mournful toll of the death knell. Some of the women began to wail.

Rhett staggered under the weight of Hedges. Seward sweated as he dragged Terry by the feet. Forrest, Scott and Bell had to make a conscious effort to slow their pace as they neared the line of women and children. Douglas hurried in the opposite direction, anxious not to miss anything.

'What we gonna do, Frank?' Seward gasped.

93

Forrest shook his head. 'One thing I can't stand, Billy, and that's lying women.'

'They sure did steer us wrong, Frank,' Bell agreed.

Forrest grinned. He halted before the line of women, who met and held his gaze across the heads of their children. 'Can't stand 'em,' he menaced. 'But I can sure lay 'em.'

'This is a house of God!' Gilda Proctor warned.

Forrest nodded to the unconscious Hedges cradled in Rhett's arms. 'God's sleepin', lady,' he said. 'So I reckon he don't care too much right now. We figure it's just a house.'

The men moved forward.

* * *

THEY marched for two hours, gaining height all the time and were almost at the snowline when Mao and the woman he had claimed went through a gap in a ridge and led the line of hostages and guards down on to the campsite.

It nestled at the foot of a shallow incline where the ground levelled out for three hundred yards before falling away again into a series of steps down to a far off river flowing through the enormous valley. The terrain was mostly of rock, dotted here and there with clumps of toughened grass and a few shrubs. But the camp, comprised of a half dozen cabins crudely constructed of stone and timber, was surrounded by an area of fertile fields bristling with rice plants, the roots of which were lost beneath the muddy surface of the water which flowed in from a clear stream. Three women worked at the edge of

94

one of the paddy fields, blocking a hole through which water was escaping.

As the newcomers neared the camp the women watched with apprehension, which slowly became resentment as their narrow eyes studied the four female hostages. They completely ignored the American men.

'You will now stop!' Shin commanded as the group moved into the compound formed by the circle of cabins.

Guards and hostages alike were grateful the long walk was over. The effort of moving forward without rest, constantly uphill, had been compounded by the thinning of the mountain air. And as they came to a halt at last, they took deep breaths, aware for the first time that the chillness stung their lungs.

'All prisoners in that hut!' Shin instructed, pointing to one of the crude buildings. 'All behave and all be treated good. Make trouble and we kill.'

Mao gave Beth's rump a final squeeze and shoved her unceremoniously towards the open door of the hut. Her expression hardened and she seemed about to hurl abuse at the Chinese for his sudden change of attitude.

'I reckon you ain't lost the chance,' Edge called to her.

The woman whirled to glare at him.

Shin stepped forward. 'One make trouble, all die.'

Beth flounced into the cabin and as the guards motioned with their shotguns, the other hostages followed her. Edge was the last to enter. The door, with a barred, glassless window, was slammed behind him and two bolts were shot home. Shin stabbed a finger at two blank-faced Chinese and they shambled forward to take up sentry positions on each side of the door.

'These Wong brothers,' Shin said, the grin back on his face. 'Very miserable men. Smile only when allowed to kill. Kill very good with knife.' Shin put his index finger against his stomach and inscribed a circle. 'Cut out belly. Not kill quick. Hurt very much.'

Edge's eyes narrowed to slits as he regarded Shin between the bars. 'You made your point,' he said.

One of the women hostages began to sob. Shin grinned more widely. 'Wongs like to cut women best. Be pleased to accommodate any lady make too much disturbance.'

He turned away, to follow Mao into a cabin on the other side of the compound. The men with the sacks of loot from the train hold-up delivered their burdens inside and emerged. Then, with the exception of the blank-faced sentries, all the Chinese men entered other huts. The women regarded the prison cabin for a few moments before returning to their work in the fields.

Edge turned and looked around the cabin, allowing his hooded eyes time to adjust to the near darkness. The barred aperture in the door was the sole source of light. The floor was rough rock, the walls dry stone and the roof unplaned timber. The area was about fifteen by ten and there was no furniture. Some of the hostages stood while others squatted or sat on the floor. It was cold in there, away from the insipid sunlight of early afternoon. Every eye was upon the tall figure of Edge, communicating a tacit agreement that he had been unanimously elected their leader. Even Beth seemed to be waiting for him to say something.

But Edge's hard-eyed stare offered no comfort or hope. He expressed nothing as he looked around the ring of pale blobs which were their faces in the murk. This rejection was too much for a middle-aged woman wearing wire-framed eye-glasses and as her spirit broke, it undammed a flood of tears and triggered a crescendo of wails.

One of the Wong brothers smashed the stock of his shotgun against the door and unleashed a babble of Chinese.

'Better shut her up,' Edge said easily. 'This ain't no bridal suite but it beats a womb with a view.'

The woman stemmed her emotions and her eyes were wide behind the spectacles as she stared at Edge.

'What kind of a man are you?' Beth snarled as she jerked free of Alvin and placed a comforting arm around the woman's shoulders.

'A poor one,' Edge replied, sinking to the floor, resting his back against the door. 'Which kinda riles me.'

He had no need to voice a threat, his tone and the menacing set of his features implying his mood. Then, with a final glance around at the wretchedness of his fellow prisoners, he closed his eyes and within moments had drifted into an easy sleep.

Chapter Six

'WHERE'D you keep the kids before you needed 'em? Forrest demanded.

Those children old enough to comprehend the danger clung to the women and began to whimper.

'Vault under the church,' Gilda Proctor replied and for the first time she revealed fear. Her voice shook.

Forrest nodded. 'Better get 'em back down there, lady.'

Many of the women stared back down the street towards the sprawled bodies of their men. Faith Terry sank teeth into her lower lip as she looked at the blood on her husband's face. It came from a meaty furrow ploughed across the top of his forehead.

The bell continued to intone its one note message of death. One of the women swayed in time with the sound, as if hypnotised.

Forrest's voice was a snarl. 'Move! You, you, you and you. Take 'em and stay with 'em.'

His rifle stabbed towards the four oldest women. Hoofbeats sounded on the street but the sergeant did not turn around to watch as Douglas led the raiders' horses up the incline. Maria Marwick rode one of the animals, her hands lashed to the saddle-horn.

'Gilda?' one of the old women pleaded.

The redhead was holding a baby. She thrust the child into the arms of the biddy. 'We tried and we lost,' she said dispiritedly. 'Now we must pay the penalty.'

Forrest showed her a leering grin. 'You got good sense, Gilda,' he complimented. 'Just keep 'em in line and nobody'll get hurt.'

' 'Cepting sleeping beauty here,' Seward hissed as he began to drag Terry closer to the church.

Faith Terry moaned and her teeth drew blood from her lip. The rest of the women handed over their children into the care of the four designated by Forrest. They were led and carried into the church. Douglas hitched the horses to the rail outside the saloon and lifted down the woman. He led her by a rope with her hands still tied.

'Not the church?' Gilda asked.

'The church,' Forrest spat at her.

Whatever spirit had been left in the women now drained from them and their shoulders drooped as they filed in through the arched doorway. The men followed. A large, brass-studded door thudded closed, blocking the entrance to the vault. The bell sounded louder within the confines of the building and they could see the old minister at the end of the aisle, pulling rhythmically on the rope.

'Enough is enough!' Forrest yelled as the women lined up against a wall.

Seward dropped Terry's legs. Rhett lowered Hedges gently onto a pew. He placed a prayer hassock under his head. The death knell stopped abruptly and the old minister peered back along the aisle through weak eyes.

'I ask forgiveness for my flock,' he said strongly. 'They spoke untruths in order to protect what they hold most dear.'

Forrest spat. 'They lied to get us killed. Now they gotta pay.'

'He sold us down the river as well, Frank,' Scott pointed out.

'And he can't pay like the dames,' Bell put in. He glanced at Rhett, grinning. 'Unless . . .'

The New Englander looked at the minister with distaste. 'You didn't want the old women,' he said with a sneer.

Forrest shrugged. 'Sorry, padre. Guess we all got to get old . . .' He swung the Spencer and squeezed the trigger . . . 'and die.'

The women screamed. The minister staggered backwards, clutching at his chest. He crashed into the altar and slid down to sit in front of it, staring down the length of his church with the glazed eyes of the dead.

'You filthy swine!' Gilda screamed.

Forrest appeared not to hear. He glanced at the troopers, resting his rifle against the rear of a pew and unbuckling his gunbelt. 'Pick your pussy,' he invited. 'Rhett, watch the rejects. They start anything, stop it.'

'You mean kill 'em, Frank?' Rhett asked.

'That'll do it,' Forrest replied.

Hedges had been swimming through the blackness towards the surface of consciousness when he had

101

been laid upon the pew. The sound of the shot jerked him fully into a pain-wracked world. For long moments he saw the vaulted roof of the church as a blurred pattern with no form, and heard the grunts and moans of rape as a distant confusion of meaningless sound. And even when full awareness came to him he could spare no thought for his surroundings. For the sickening pain in his head and the burning agony in his leg kept him locked inside his own world of self-pity.

But pain, if not an old friend, was a familiar companion and within a short time he had adjusted to the misery. Memory returned, thrusting into his mind every detail of what had happened up to the time the bullet found its mark. He explored the ridge of bruising on his forehead and then his probing fingers ran over the hard caked blood crusting his pants around the thigh wound. Satisfied that this was the extent of his injuries, he hauled himself into a sitting position and slitted his eyes to look over the back of the pew.

He saw Rhett aiming a rifle from the hip towards a cluster of five trembling women. He saw five other women, sprawled naked upon the tattered remnants of their clothes, arms and legs spread wide in unresisting submission as their bodies were assaulted by the lustful troopers. And he saw the murderer of the only woman he had ever loved.

Again, the Captain retreated into a world of his own. But this time he took another with him. Pain, although it was necessarily a component of this world, was forced back to the periphery, to act as a barrier against outside influence. Thus, as he stood up and moved out of the pew, using his hands to swing his injured leg, he was immune to the sights and sounds of the brutal orgy.

'Captain!' Rhett shouted, drawing the attention of his charges to Hedges' clumsy progress.

Hedges did not hear the trooper's startled voice as he reached his objective and stood, swaying, staring hate down at the unconscious Terry. Scott and Douglas expended their lust and rolled clear of their victims. The women attempted to cover themselves, drawing up their knees and clutching arms across their bruised breasts. The two troopers scrambled to their feet, buckling their belts and snatching up their rifles. Forrest, Seward and Bell thrust to the conclusion of their acts and immediately became aware of the hatred emanating from Hedges to fill the church. Faith Terry, who had suffered the onslaught of Seward's cruel desires was unmindful of her nakedness as she rose into a kneeling posture and clasped her hands together beneath her chin.

'Haven't you done enough?' she implored.

The voice of a woman was able to penetrate Hedges' private world of hate and, once punctured, the shell peeled completely away. The Captain looked up from the unconscious man and his hooded eyes raked the faces of all who were watching him.

Forrest finished buckling on his gunbelt and snatched up his Spencer. 'You want us to take care of him, Captain?' he asked. 'You don't look so good.'

Hedges' voice was a croak. 'You look shagged out yourself.' He turned his cruel-eyed stare towards the kneeling woman. 'He burned my girl.'

103

Faith Terry's green eyes implored mercy. 'Please,' she whispered. 'Revenge won't bring her back.'

'I ain't that ambitious, lady,' Hedges replied, glancing around the church. His hooded eyes rested upon the altar with the dead minister resting against it and the bell rope hanging down in front.

'String him up and wake him up,' he ordered. 'About ten feet. Horizontal.'

Forrest began to grin, then looked confused.

'Flat out,' Hedges amplified. 'Face down.'

All the women save Faith Terry clustered into a group, those still fully dressed moving to the fore to hide their companions' nakedness. The wife of the unconscious raider sank lower on to her knees and rested her forehead on the stone floor. She began to sob softly. While Rhett continued to stand guard over the women, the other troopers lifted Terry and carried him to the altar. They stacked pews one atop another to gain height and held the unconscious man aloft as Forrest wound the bell rope around his limp body. The bell tolled once as the rope took the strain and Terry's body swung freely, held by loops around his ankles, middle and shoulders.

Seward went into the vestry and emerged a few moments later carrying a pail slopping water. Hedges, his lean, hollow-eyed face set in a mask of evil intent, limped along the aisle. Behind him Faith Terry's sobs became wails. The Captain nodded to Seward. The youngster giggled and hurled the water up into the blood-run face of the raider. The man's body jerked and he groaned.

'Build a fire,' Hedges ordered.

Scott began to tear hymn books and Bibles. Bell, Douglas and Seward used their rifle stocks to smash a pew into kindling wood. Forrest nodded towards the dead minister.

'What about him, Captain?'

'He'll burn,' Hedges answered.

'Yeah,' Seward agreed excitedly. 'Real good.'

Terry groaned again and snapped open his eyes as screwed up paper and wood was piled around the dead minister. Pews were upended and stacked around the altar.

'You'll all rot in hell!' Gilda Proctor screamed.

'We've already booked our tickets, ma'am,' Rhett told her as Hedges nodded to Forrest, who struck a match on the stone floor and tossed it into the centre of the pyre.

The torn books ignited immediately and within moments the dry, shattered wood became willing fuel for the fire. Terry screamed and twisted his head around to stare at the half circle of troopers.

'Cut me down, for Christ's sake!' he shrieked, and coughed as grey woodsmoke billowed around him.

'You remember me, Terry?' Hedges snarled at him.

'Yeah. Yeah. I remember.'

The wood began to crackle, then to roar. The flames licked hungrily at the leaning pews.

'An eye for an eye!' Hedges shouted as Terry began to struggle and his body revolved at the end of the rope.

'Oh dear God, end it!' a woman pleaded.

The flames found and consumed the robe of the dead minister and then licked across his waxy flesh.

They seared deep and the cloying sweetness of charred meat filled the church. The billowing clouds changed from grey to black, completely engulfing the suspended man whose body was wracked by a coughing fit.

'Will you look at that!' Seward yelled.

'Yeah,' Rhett called in reply. 'Holy smoke!'

'Let me . . . !' Terry managed to scream before the oily smoke caught his throat again.

Then his cries took on the timbre of pain rather than terror as the heat of the blaze reached him, scorching his face. Sparks exploded upwards and lodged in his clothes. A dozen tiny fires sprang into being, rapidly expanding. Terry's screams merged into one continuous sound that resounded across the stifling church and was suddenly curtailed as his body was enveloped in a yellow glow. For long moments it was a flaring apparition dripping flames amid the billowing smoke. Then the rope around his middle snapped and he sagged. The binding at ankles and shoulders parted in the same instant and the charred body dropped, sprawling across the top of the altar.

Faith Terry dragged her head up, stared hysterically along the aisle and then fell sideways, saliva slobbering from her soundlessly working mouth.

'Put it out,' Hedges ordered suddenly, after long moments of staring at the blackened body, hardly recognisable as a human form.

Seward snatched up the pail, ran into the vestry and reappeared to slosh water on to the fire. Other troopers moved forward to stamp out the final few flames among the ashes.

106

'Score settled, Captain?' Forrest asked.

Pain came to the forefront of Hedges' mind once again and he had to lean against the side of a pew to keep from falling. 'I reckon,' he said.

'What about the women? There's some more, and some kids down in the vault.'

Hedges shook his head. 'Now, enough is enough,' he rasped, clutching his injured leg.

'They'll finger us,' Forrest insisted.

'We're a long way from anyplace,' Hedges replied, tensing his body against the waves of pain which were threatening to swamp him. 'Go make sure they have to walk if they do go there.'

Forrest nodded and headed back down the aisle. The other troopers followed him, anxious to leave behind the sickly sweetness of the air inside the church. Hedges limped along in their wake. He had not covered half the distance to the sunlit doorway when a volley of pistol shots rang out, closely followed by another. Dead horseflesh thudded into the ground. The malice in the women's eyes was like a physical force turned against him. On the floor, writhing in her madness, Faith Terry clawed at her naked flesh with hands formed into demented claws. Trails of fresh blood traced ugly patterns across her white skin.

'You didn't have to do it!' Gilda Proctor screeched, flinging off a restraining hand.

Hoofbeats sounded out on the street. Hedges limped to the doorway and turned to look back down the aisle, to where the charred body of Terry hung across the altar like a blackened sack.

'There's a war on, lady,' he rasped. 'We all got to make sacrifices.'

He stumbled out into the sunlight.

*   *   *

WITH the coming of night, the mountain air grew colder and many of the prisoners in the cabin huddled close together for warmth: perhaps for comfort, too. And even those whose dignity forbade such an overt sign of their moral or physical wretchedness moved closer to the main group, hugging themselves or blowing on their hands.

The lone exception was Edge, who maintained his position close to the door, alternately sleeping and waking: hearing, but not attempting to look for the cause of each sound coming in from the compound. Thus, when darkness fell, he was aware that the guard had been changed three times, the Chinese had eaten two meals without feeding their hostages and had lit a fire at the centre of the encirclement of cabins. But when he heard a clink of bottles and noted the chatter of the Chinese was rising to high excitement, interspersed with gusts of laughter, he got to his feet. He began to pace up and down in the confined space, flexing his muscles and breathing hard against his hands. The frightened eyes of his fellow-prisoners followed each movement. The woman with the eye-glasses started to make dry sobbing noises.

'Shush, Mrs. White,' Beth consoled, pulling the woman's face against her ample bosom.

Edge, satisfied his circulation was as good as it was going to get in the icy conditions, ceased his pacing and went to the door to peer out between the bars. The guards sensed his presence and looked at him blankly. Edge ignored them.

The sky was clear and a half moon augmented by a myriad jewel-like stars turned the rugged mountain country into a wonderland of glistening peaks and mysterious shadows. But in the forefront of this natural grandeur man was an ugly intrusion. The Chinese sat in a circle around the blazing log fire, minus their coolie hats so that their greasy hair plaited at the back into pigtails glistened in the dancing flames. A half dozen bottles passed back and forth along each arc forming the circle, the men sucking greedily at the necks. Mao and Shin sat side-by-side, with a bottle each. In the background, silhouetted against the dull greyness of a flooded rice paddy, the three women looked on, the statue-like stiffness of their posture suggesting controlled anger.

After awhile, as the chatter became more high-pitched and the laughter more frequent, one of the drinkers took a harmonica from under his robe and began to blow against it. He produced a tuneless wail, but a half-dozen drunken Chinese were moved to jump to their feet. They began to stagger around the compound in a parody of a dance, drawing cheers from their companions.

'What's happening, Mr. Edge?' Alvin asked.

'Local hop,' Edge replied flatly. 'They ain't good, but they got a lot of spirit.'

He concentrated his scrutiny upon Mao and Shin as the leader and his lieutenant put their heads together and exchanged words. Then Mao clapped his

109

hands, the crack silencing the harmonica player and curtailing the drunken dance. Shin rose and approached the prison cabin, the familiar grin back on his round face.

'Now what?' Beth asked in the sudden silence.

'Mao's had another thought,' Edge replied. 'I figure it's a dirty one.'

Shin halted in front of the door. His smiling eyes locked with Edge's cold stare. From his position of strength, the young Chinese refused to be provoked. He bowed in a mocking manner.

'Mr Mao never *jig-jig* with Occidental lady,' Shin said, his voice only slightly slurred. 'Some other men here not have pleasure. They intrigued.'

Edge curled back his lips in a grin. 'Railroad tracks run the same way all round the world,' he said.

'We no that stupid,' Shin said. 'Still wish *jig-jig*. You send out women. They good, we turn all you loose.'

Mrs White started to wail again. Two other women—a plain teenager with a blotched complexion and a thin maiden lady—pressed themselves against the rear wall of the cabin. Beth laid a calming hand over Alvin's lips as he opened his mouth to protest.

Shin nodded to the guards, who stepped back, levelling their shotguns at the door. Then Shin stepped forward and shot back the two securing bolts. 'They no come out by time count ten, you all dead. Bang bang. No place to run in cabin. We get other Occidental ladies some other place!'

As the door swung open, Edge stepped back out

110

of the entrance. He looked at the pale faces of the women.

'One,' Shin said.

'You're sitting on our survival,' Edge urged.

'Two.'

'Beth!' Alvin cried, reaching for the woman.

'Three.'

'We're no good to each other dead,' she pointed out, jerking free of his grip and standing, pulling Mrs White to her feet.

'Four.'

Beth looked over each shoulder at the two other women and jerked her head.

'Five.'

They stood and stepped through the helplessly shocked men. Beth led them towards the doorway.

'Six.'

'Beth!' Alvin pleaded again, reaching out a hand. A man knocked it down.

'Seven.'

Beth emerged from the cabin. Mrs White halted and turned pleading eyes towards Edge. 'They're heathens,' she said. 'How do we know they'll keep their word?'

'Eight.'

'Two more and we'll never get the chance to find out.'

Mrs White swallowed hard and stepped from the cabin. The teenager and the spinster stumbled after her. Shin barked an order and the door was slammed shut, the bolts shot home.

Mao's voice chattered and the harmonica player blew into his instrument again. The prisoners jostled

Edge, trying to peer around him for a view through the bars. Shin bowed to the women, gesturing with a hand that they should go towards the fire. As they did so, Beth with her head held high, her body swaying, the other three shambling behind her, Edge glanced across to where he had last seen the Chinese women. They were no longer in sight.

Mao spoke again and Shin pumped his head and broadened his grin.

'Mr Mao think men dance badly. Think you be much better.'

Mrs White wailed her misery and Shin shook his head violently.

'No say sing. Say dance. Like this.'

He clasped his hands high over his head and executed an inelegant hip-swivelling motion. The men clapped their hands gleefully and exploded with high-pitched laughter. All except Mao, who took out his knife and began to rake dirt from under his nails. Shin completed his demonstration and his face became sad as he looked at the women.

'Chinese patience soon run out,' he warned. 'You do like I say or men go to meet honorable ancestors.'

Beth's angular features looked even more sensuous in the flickering firelight. 'You said you'd let us go if nobody followed from the train.'

Shin nodded in agreement. 'That is correct. But first must please men. Dance, then *jig-jig*.'

'I don't know how to do a jig!' the blotchy-faced teenager whined.

'That part's got nothing to do with dancing.' Beth told her, and began to sway her hips.

Her movements completely ignored the tuneless

112

rasp from the harmonica and her body swayed as if to some rhythm from within herself. She thrust her hands high into the air, emphasising the swells of her breasts and as her feet began to move the men started to clap out a timing. The other three women watched her in amazement for several seconds, then tried to imitate her. But they were not dancehall girls and whatever natural feminine gracefulness they may have possessed was held in check by the harsh grip of fear. They moved like stiff-limbed sleep-walkers, bumping into each other, sometimes tripping over their own feet.

But the men, alternately applauding and sucking rice wine from the bottles, were unconcerned with technique. The surrender of the women into the enforced entertainment had a stimulating effect upon the Chinese as they savoured the ultimate delight.

When Mao held up a hand the men became abruptly quiet. Even the harmonica player ceased his monotonous noise.

'You keep dancing,' Shin barked at the women as they faltered. He had remained standing, but now he moved back to his place beside Mao and sank to the ground, crossing his legs. He nodded his approval as the women's bodies continued to gyrate in the silence, disturbed only by the crackling of the fire and the swish of their petticoats. 'Now you have choice,' he continued. 'You take off clothes or men remove them for you. Men sometimes not gentle in disrobing ladies.'

'We've got to stop it!' Alvin said hoarsely, his face twisted into ugliness by frustrated fury.

'I'm open to suggestions,' Edge replied softly.

113

'Talk to them!' Alvin pleaded, elbowing his way through the press of bodies to reach Edge at the door. 'Promise them anything.'

Edge shook his head, his hooded eyes moving from Beth to the other women as their fingers reached for the fastenings on their gowns. 'Right now they got everything they want, kid.'

The hush in the night seemed to expand and take on substance as the fingers of the women fumbled with buttons and hooks. The youngest girl and Mrs White were crying silently, firelight glistening its reflection from the tears streaming down their cheeks. The thin woman had her eyes tight shut and her lips set in a rigid line which showed up almost black against the paleness of her skin. Beth, perhaps despite herself, could not prevent the experience of a lifetime adding an easy grace to her actions.

Edge heard the deep breathing of the guards flanking the doorway, then the scrape of their boots against the hard ground as they moved closer to the women. They took several more steps as the top of Beth's dress fell away from her body, exposing her full breasts, creamy white in the firelight. Grunts and gasps escaped from the throats of the Chinese as they leered at the naked flesh. The teenager's dress fell next, floating to the ground with no waistline to support it. Fear and cold set her body trembling as it swayed and her fingers were blue as they fumbled with the flimsy underwear. Then her youthful slimness was naked and she dropped her arms, vainly trying to cover herself.

'Arms up!' Shin barked, his eyes no longer smiling as they drank in the curves and hollows of the trem-

114

ulous flesh. He held out a hand and rotated it. 'And turn.'

Sobbing, the girl complied. Beth's voluptuous body was bared before the lust of the Chinese. Then the thin woman's, finally the flaccidness of Mrs. White's flesh. The guards moved in closer. The dance continued, each ripple of exposed flesh building up a greater degree of tense expectancy.

'Faster!' Shin demanded, and began to clap his hands. The others joined him, matching his cadence: measured at first, but getting faster by the moment. The incessant sound seemed to induce a near-trance in the women and they flung themselves about wildly to keep time.

A shadowy figure moved lithely across the doorway of the prison cabin and the two bolts grated out of their brackets. A round face, which might have been pretty had the eyes shown intelligence, looked in at Edge through the bars. He had to lip-read against the clapping which was now a continuous tumult.

'*You no say I set free.*'

Edge nodded and the girl ducked out of sight and flitted away to go behind the circle of cabins. He turned to look into the pale faces of the hostages.

'What is it?' Alvin asked.

'Chink dames figure they got the entertainment franchise up here. Door's open.'

Alvin pressed forward. 'Let's rush the bastards.'

Edge's right hand streaked to the back of his neck and moved down, flashing metal. Alvin gulped as the point of the razor pricked his throat. His body became rigid. The other prisoners backed away.

'Kill yourself some other time, Alvin,' Edge hissed. 'Right now, listen—and listen good.'

The noise of the clapping hands was driving the women close to the point of exhaustion and even Beth had lost her rhythm. Their heads rolled from side to side, their arms flapped limply and their legs bowed and buckled. But as the humiliating dance grew more grotesque, so the excitement of the drunken Chinese was heightened.

The thin woman collapsed first, and at once a man threw himself upon her, his hands clawing at her meagre breasts. She screamed and found strength to rain blows upon him. He laughed and hit her back-handed across the cheek.

Edge pushed open the door of the cabin and slid out, pressing himself against the wall. Alvin followed him, then the other prisoners. Edge and Alvin stayed where they were while the rest worked their way around to the rear of the cabin and then moved off towards the other buildings surrounding the compound.

Mrs White sank to the ground, tried to raise herself, but toppled sideways. The Wong brothers scuttled away from the group and leered down at the quivering woman. Each raised his robe and the woman screamed in terror as she saw their naked readiness beneath.

Edge and Alvin moved forward, into the area illuminated by the firelight. But no eye was turned in their direction. The attention of every Chinese was torn between the two remaining dancers and the women writhing on the ground. Alvin held back, two feet behind one of the guards. Edge closed in and halted, his body a fraction of an inch from that of the second guard. The razor handle nestled along the centre of his palm, the blade concealed by his fingers. He raised his arm and his shirt cuff brushed the shoulder of the Chinese. The man's head snapped around, his eyes widening. Edge's free hand curved around the other side of the man and closed over the stock of the shotgun. Edge grinned at him and drew the blade across his throat. He jerked the shotgun from the dead grip. The barrels were shiny with blood that had gushed from the slashed jugular vein.

The other guard heard the thud of the body and started to turn. He froze when he saw the tall half-breed covering him with the shotgun. He did not resist when Alvin stepped up to him and pulled his own weapon from his grasp.

Beth and the girl crumpled to the ground and the clapping stopped instantly. Edge nodded to Alvin. The boy hesitated but a moment, then thrust his gun into the belly of the guard and squeezed the trigger. The man screamed and was flipped over backwards. Blood spurted like a muddy spring from his ghastly wound.

'Party's over!' Edge yelled, his voice cutting across the sudden babble of Chinese, silencing it. He aimed the shotgun at Mao. Other hostages emerged from the cabins, encircling the men around the fire. Each held a shotgun. The only Chinese to move were those who had claimed the exhausted women. They backed away from their prizes.

Shin forced a grin to his face. 'We let you go now,' he said.

117

'Obliged,' Edge said. 'Get dressed now, ladies. You did okay but these guys don't feel up to it no more.'

The women scrambled on to all fours and scuttled to pick up their clothes, and dress. Relief undammed fresh tears. They hurried to move outside the circle of freed hostages.

Mao unloosed a rapid fire rattle of Chinese. Shin nodded and looked across at Edge.

'Mr Mao wishes to know how you escape?'

'We had help from the green-eyed monster. A fink among the Chinks.'

Shin was confused. 'I no understand.'

'Tell your boss and let him work it out. He's the big thinker around here. Now tell these guys to get in the pokey.' He motioned with the shotgun towards the prison cabin.

'You have permission to go,' Mao said. 'No need lock us up.'

'One,' Edge said easily.

Shin received the message immediately. He passed it on to the men in their own language, then started towards the cabin with the barred door. Some of the men rose to follow him.

'Two,' Edge counted.

'It going to be tight squeeze for us,' Shin complained.

'I feel for you,' Edge told him. 'Three.'

Shin hurried into the cabin. Ten of the men followed him. The remainder continued to squat on the ground, looking to Mao for guidance.

'Off your butt, crud,' Edge spat at the gang's leader.

Mao bowed from his sitting posture, then began

118

to rise, slowly. The others unfolded their legs. Abruptly, Mao shot out a hand, grasped a burning log from the fire and whirled. Edge squeezed one of the shotgun triggers and the load turned the man's head into a crimson pulp. But the log was already spinning through the air and even before the dead man had hit the ground it had sailed into the open doorway of his cabin.

'Lock 'em in!' Edge yelled to Alvin as the Chinese in the compound exploded into movement, hands jerking knives from beneath their robes.

The boy shouldered the door closed and shot home the bolts. Knives spun through the firelight and three of the hostages screamed their death cries as honed steel penetrated vital organs. Then the moment of shock was gone and shotguns blazed. Robed bodies crumpled, spraying blood and torn flesh into the fire. The fire sizzled and gave off tiny puffs of steam.

An eerie, post-violence hush fell upon the compound. A shout shattered it.

'The money!'

Some of the freed hostages dropped their empty shotguns and ran towards Mao's cabin. But an orange glow from within emitted a fierce heat to drive them back. Alvin rushed to Beth's side and gripped both her hands, babbling incoherently.

'Hey, we could die in here if you leave us,' Shin called softly through the bars.

'You're one smart Chink,' Edge told him. 'You catch on fast.' He glanced around at his fellow hostages. 'You ready to pull out?'

They took a final look at the blazing cabin and

119

moved dispiritedly across the compound to join the half-breed. Each of the hurriedly-dressed women was supported by a man. Some of the men, deeply shocked by the carnage they left behind, looked ready to keel over themselves.

'What about burying them?' a grey-haired man asked. 'At least the three we lost.'

'Reckon it'll make 'em feel any better?' Edge asked.

'It'll make me feel better,' the man responded.

Edge shrugged and started up the slope away from the compound. The others fell in behind him and the grey-haired man held back for only a few moments before joining the rear of the column. They moved silently until they went between the gap in the ridge over-looking the campsite. Then Mrs White found it impossible to check her emotions further and her body-wracking sobs punctured the stillness.

'What the hell's wrong now?' Edge snarled.

'How can you ask that?' Beth retorted. 'You saw what she went through back there.'

'Sure,' Edge told her. 'Mrs White had a rough time, but all she lost was a little dignity.'

'A little dignity!' Beth raged. 'Those two Chinese . . .'

'Showed her the goods but didn't deliver,' Edge cut in. He bared his teeth in a grin. 'Two Wongs didn't get to make a White.'

Chapter Seven

FED but not rested, their morale boosted by a sur-
feit of sex and killing, the six troopers rode hard in
the wake of the injured Hedges. Steeling himself
against the rising tide of pain, the Captain led them
north along the turnpike for several miles, before
swinging to the west across untilled countryside. He
rode with only one foot in the stirrup, the injured
leg hanging free to prevent the crusting of congealed
blood from cracking and opening the wound to dust.

Not until mid-afternoon did he call a halt, when
he judged they had put fifteen miles between themselves and the town without men. He chose the spot
because clear, ice cold water bubbled up from a
spring and a screen of trees provided both shade and
cover to the south and east. To the west the terrain
was open and undulating, offering them a broad
vista in which to spot movement. To the north a
line of verdant hills dominated the horizon.

'We gonna get some sleep at last?' Forrest asked
as he slid from his mount. He stretched out on the
lush grass and pressed his mouth into the spring
water.

The other men dismounted and waited their turn.
Nobody offered to help Hedges from his horse. He
slid out of the saddle clumsily and his injured leg

thudded to the ground. The blackened blood began to ooze with fresh scarlet. His lean face was twisted by an agony he fought against voicing.

'After you've earned it,' he croaked as Forrest finished drinking his fill and rolled over onto his back.

'How's that, Captain?' the sergeant asked.

'First you're gonna dig this slug out of my leg.'

Forrest sat up, an evil grin pasted on his features. 'Be a pleasure, sir,' he said.

'Figured you'd enjoy it,' Hedges replied, unfastening his tunic, then his belt. 'You ever done it before?'

Forrest nodded. 'Down on the border. Buddy of mine caught a lawman's bullet in his shoulder.'

'Didn't know you had any friends,' Hedges said, grimacing as he lifted himself and rolled his pants down. When he came to the area of the wound he wrenched the material away from the dried blood.

'He was the only one,' Forrest replied easily, taking the neckerchief Hedges handed him and pushing Rhett away from the spring so he could soak it. 'But then he turned against me. Wound turned septic and he had to have his arm off.'

Hedges pressed his hands hard against the ground and stared up into the unmarred blueness of the sky as Forrest cleaned off the congealed blood. The wound was in the fleshy part of the thigh, out of line with any bone. Cleaned of blood, it was just a neat hole puffed with an angry-looking red surrounding.

'I'm gonna need your blade, Captain,' Forrest said.

Hedges leaned his head forward. 'Take it.'

The sergeant slid the razor from its pouch and

tested its sharpness against his thumb. 'Ain't honed like it should be,' he said.

'Oughta make it more fun for you,' Hedges hissed. 'Just make sure it's clean—and your hands.'

Forrest held Hedges' pain-filled stare for a moment, then nodded and moved to the spring. The men had drunk their fill and looked down at Hedges with an utter lack of compassion.

'Give me all the matches you got, then unsaddle the horses,' Forrest barked.

The troopers surrendered their matches and then attended to the horses. Forrest wrung his hands in the spring water, then crouched down beside Hedges. He pulled the Captain's belt out of his pants and gave it to him.

'To bite on,' he said, and struck a match on Hedges' boot sole, then ran the blade through the flame. 'I'll make it quick as I can.'

'Just make it good,' Hedges countered.

Forrest shook out the match and moved to strike another. But instead, he whirled to face Hedges and smashed a right cross into the Captain's jaw. Hedges' body stretched its full length across the grass.

'Jesus,' Rhett exclaimed.

'Billy!' Forrest snapped. 'Stand over him. He looks like coming out of it before I finish, let him have another one.'

The youngster giggled and squatted beside Hedges, opposite Forrest. He balled his fist, ready. Forrest used one more match, then inserted the blade into the wound. Fresh blood spurted. New sweat broke out on the faces of Forrest and his audience. The sergeant moved the razor back and forth, exploring the hole. He grunted as his probing located the bullet.

'Ain't deep,' he murmured.

The wound was now erupting dark blood like red lava and he was working blind. His wrist suddenly moved and the bullet was flipped out onto the grass.

'How about that,' Seward said in awe.

'Clean him up,' Forrest ordered. 'And bind it.'

The sergeant sat down under a tree and lit a cigarette, watching impassively as Seward and Rhett attended to the wound. The hole was now twice as large as it had been. Rhett surrendered his undervest without argument and this was rinsed and torn into strips to form a bandage.

Hedges regained consciousness with a low groan and his hands clawed towards his thigh, which felt as though it were on fire. He was fully dressed again, the razor was back in the neck pouch and Seward was grinning at him, holding out the damaging bullet between finger and thumb.

'Memento, Captain?' he asked.

Pain coated Hedges' face with sweat that immediately crusted in the heat and streaked the stubbled skin with salt lines.

'Get rid of it, Billy,' Forrest rasped. 'He don't need reminding.'

They remained beside the spring until the heat had gone from the afternoon and the level of the Captain's agony had subsided. All were aware—but did not voice an opinion—that Hedges' wound was still dangerous and would remain so until it had received medical attention. And, as the one most deeply concerned, it was Hedges himself who gave the order to mount up and continue the ride north.

The pain returned to its full intensity as Scott and Rhett helped him up on to his horse and subsided hardly at all as he led the troopers at an easy canter across the open country. They rode throughout the rest of the afternoon and into evening, on a curved course that took them to the west and then north, swinging wide of Atlanta. Water was plentiful, and so was food in the many small settlements dotting the foothills of the Blue Mountain range. But Hedges kept the men hungry until nightfall. Then he organised, but took no part in, a raid on a grocery and feed store of a hamlet straddling the Coosa River.

Forrest handled the foray with the skill of an expert thief and the men were able to clatter out of town across the north-bound river bridge without pursuit. They carried with them a sufficient horde of supplies to last them for two days. But Hedges could not meet the schedule. As they made camp and ate their newly acquired rations some five miles north of the river, the Captain became aware of a numbness in his injured leg. The lack of feeling provided a moment of sweet relief, but Hedges did not allow himself to be deluded by the sudden cessation of pain. For he was experienced in the results of untreated wounds. Thus, as he removed the dressing, he was prepared for the nauseating odour of decayed flesh and the sight of swollen green-tinged pus that told of gangrene.

'You knew I weren't no sawbones,' Forrest defended as he saw the festering wound in the blue moonlight.

'I ain't making no complaint,' Hedges answered. He pointed into the darkness. 'North's that way, over the mountains. Union ought to have Tennessee buttoned up by now. But don't forget you got on Confederate threads.'

The troopers eyed the Captain in confusion. Forrest was the first to see the light.

'You asking us to leave you here, Captain?'

'Bother you?'

Forrest nodded. 'Maybe it does. I ain't never known you give up on anything till now.'

'I ain't giving up,' Hedges replied. 'I figure to find me a doctor and keep my leg from rotting off. That'll take time. By then you could be back in blue and fighting the war again.'

The troopers were neutrals and none spoke in an attempt to influence Forrest as the sergeant pondered the decision. Only crickets disturbed the silence as he thought. Finally he shook his head.

'You ain't no friend of mine, Captain,' he said softly. 'I figure I've had good reason to kill you a dozen times. But I didn't. And you know why? I need you. I hate your cruddy guts and I'd like to put a bullet in your other leg. But I ain't sure I could get where I'm goin' without you.' He looked around at the impassive faces of the troopers. 'Billy, scout ahead in the hills. See if you can find a town big enough to have a sawbones. Rog—rip up your underwear and make a new bandage for the Captain.'

Seward mounted and rode off. Bell started to unbutton his tunic. Hedges showed Forrest a cold grin.

'You're making a bad decision, Forrest,' he said softly.

126

'Maybe,' the sergeant replied without looking at the wounded man. 'But I need you around to keep making the right ones.'

Hedges' expression revealed nothing of what he was thinking as he allowed Bell to rebind the wound and he held his silence as he was lifted up into the saddle. They had travelled less than half a mile when Seward approached them at the gallop.

'You find a place?' Forrest demanded as the youngster drew in deep breaths.

'Sure thing,' Seward shot back, pointing to a ridge in the north east. 'Big enough for a dozen medics, I reckon.'

'Ain't nothin' that big till Chattanooga,' Hedges said coldly, glancing at the star dotted sky, checking his bearings.

'But this ain't no town, sir,' Seward replied with a grin.

'You said big,' Forrest snarled.

'Yeah,' Seward answered, whirling his horse and heeling it forward. 'Big on trouble, maybe. Come take a look.'

Cursing Seward's obtuseness, the rest of the horsemen streamed after him up a grassy slope featured with clumps of trees and weather-smoothed rocks. At the crest they halted and looked down in amazement at a shallow valley containing a sight with which all were familiar.

'It's a goddam army camp!' Douglas said in a hushed whisper.

'And how,' Bell put in.

Hedges' slitted eyes raked across the moonlit vista below, realising it was more than a mere camp. For

127

this was only half of it, with rigidly straight lines of tents, a timber headquarters building and a drill area. But on the other side of a road which bisected the valley the land was host to an ordnance and supply depot. Crowded close together were rows of artillery pieces, wagons, powder magazines, small arms and ammunition stores, feed barns, a corral crowded with horses and—in one corner—a wire mesh stockade. As the Union troopers looked on, a line of slaves was being urged through the open gate of the stockade. Other Negroes continued to work under armed guard in various sections of the depot.

'Your decision, Captain,' Forrest said lightly.

'An easy one,' Hedges replied, using his good leg to urge the horse forward. 'I ain't got no choice.'

'You'll do the talkin'?' the sergeant called after him.

Hedges looked back over his shoulder. 'We got chased out of Tennessee by the Yankees,' he answered. 'Anyone wants to know the details, you just tagged along after me.' He forced a grin. 'I'm the only one among us knows his ass from his elbow.'

'Ain't that the truth,' Scott muttered and ducked under a back-handed cuff from Forrest before the troopers moved off in the wake of the Captain.

Only the stockade and the corral were fenced in, but sentries were posted at intervals around the perimeter of the camp and its adjacent depot. Two infantry privates flanked the heavily rutted road where it passed between the end of the first row of tents and a cluster of 4½-inch calibre brass cannon. They offered no overt threat with their carbines.

Hedges halted his horse and pointed to his blood-

128

soaked pants leg. 'Got me a bad one, soldier,' he said. 'Can I get it fixed here?'

One of the sentries nodded. 'Sure enough. Hospital tent's down beyond the command post.'

'Obliged,' Hedges replied. 'Didn't know about this place.'

The second sentry spat. 'Weren't here two weeks ago, sarge. Rosecrans's pushed Bragg back to Chattanooga and Bragg's screaming for reinforcement and supplies to keep the Yankees crossing the Tennessee. Don't reckon no bum leg's gonna keep you outta the fight.'

'Hear it'll be over by Christmas,' Hedges said as he moved on down the road.

Both sentries spat now, considering the familiar remark unworthy of further response. Hedges waited until they were out of earshot, riding between a row of single storey magazines and the tents of a cavalry regiment. Flickering camp fires augmented the moonlight but none of the Confederate soldiers moving about their evening chores gave the newcomers a second glance.

'Look and remember,' Hedges muttered to the troopers. 'All this stuff gets moved up to Bragg, Old Rosy won't stand a chance.'

'What are we supposed to do about it?' Rhett complained.

'Like the Captain says,' Forrest hissed. 'Look and remember.'

'But—'

'I didn't say anything about yakking,' Hedges rasped as they went in front of the headquarters' building with

129

its pole flying the thirteen starred Rebel flag. 'There's a war on, Rhett. Careless talk costs lives.'

They halted outside a large tent marked HOSPITAL.

* * *

THE escaped hostages reached the railroad in the cold grey light of a new dawn and sat on the ties between the rails. After awhile the strain of their ordeal at the mountain encampment and the exhausting walk down from the high peaks overtook even the strongest of them and they slept.

Even Edge, a man whose experience of life left him immune to suffering and who had taken his rest in the prison cabin, closed his eyes against the first rays of the sun and allowed his mind and body to submit to the encroachment of sleep.

The humming of the rails woke him first and he was at the side of the stream, splashing icy water onto his stubbled face when the approach of the train roused the others. It was an east-bound freight and as it reached the top of the grade and entered the ravine the engineer was preparing to open the throttle and make good time through the mountains and down on to the central plain of Nevada.

But he did a double-take towards the knot of people at the side of the track and jerked at the brake lever. Edge ambled across to join the others as the big locomotive ground to a halt beside them.

'Holy cow!' the engineer gasped. 'You the folks taken off by the Chinamen?'

'You hear about that?' Edge drawled.

'You bet we heard,' the fireman shot back in high

130

excitement. 'Telegraph ain't stopped humming with the news.'

'Seems no one was humming to come out and rescue us,' a man complained bitterly.

Neither crewman was provoked by the comment. The engineer shrugged. 'Them Chinamen must have taken fifty people off the trains. Ain't a one of 'em bin seen again. Just too much mountain to search. How'd you get loose?'

'It's a long story,' Beth said with a sigh.

'With music,' Edge put in. 'About how she was almost made in the mountains.'

The woman and Alvin glared at him hatefully.

'Bound for Chicago by way of Salt Lake City, Cheyenne and Omaha,' the engineer announced. 'Can't offer you no Pullman comfort, but you can help yourself to oranges in the first boxcar.'

Edge nodded and started off along the side of the train. The others trailed him and hoisted themselves up through the open door of a car. One end was stacked with orange crates, the scent of the fruit cloying the air. As soon as the last man had hauled himself aboard, the engineer sounded a blast on the whistle and the train jerked forward.

Initially, Edge was the only one to feel hunger, and satisfy it by breaking open a crate and eating a half dozen oranges. But as the train's speed increased and the steady clicking of the wheels against the track injected a sense of security into the others, they, too, accepted the engineer's invitation. Suddenly ravenous, they gorged themselves on the fruit.

Nobody talked and when an hour had passed, the

131

weather getting warmer with the downhill rush of the train, most slipped into a secure sleep. Edge was sitting at the open door, his feet swinging freely in the slipstream, his mind impassively considering the loss of his stake.

'Mr Edge,' Alvin said, close behind him.

The half-breed turned and studied the pale faces of the boy and the woman crouched at his side. 'You want something?'

Alvin cleared his throat. 'I know about Beth's past. Everybody in Redwood City knows she was a dancehall girl and . . .' He glanced at Beth.

'And a whore,' she said for him, her eyes holding Edge's gaze levelly.

Alvin pumped his head. 'Right. But that don't make no difference to me. It does to my father, which is why we had to run off. . . .'

Again his voice trailed away. Edge clicked his tongue against the back of his teeth. 'You askin' me somethin', Alvin?' he asked. 'You want me to be best man at your weddin'?'

'You ain't even a . . .' Beth hissed, but held back as Alvin laid a restraining hand on her arm.

'It's just that I'd like you to stop insulting Beth, Mr Edge.' His facial muscles were tight, pulling his pale skin taut over his cheekbones. 'I told you I'm not much with a gun. But if you keep saying—'

'Hold it, Alvin,' Edge cut in. His eyes narrowed and his lips curled back. 'I got the message. Back it up with a threat and . . .'

'Oh, my God. Look what they did?'

Beth's voice was hoarse with shock and her face

132

was twisted by horror a moment before she turned away and began to vomit the oranges she had eaten.

Edge and Alvin looked out through the open doorway. The train was swaying around a curve in the foothills and they could see across to the far side of an expanse of low brush where the railroad cut into a stand of pines. A body was strung upside down by a rope, bowing a low branch with its weight. At first it seemed to be cloaked in a skintight garment, coal black and outlining every rise and plane, leaving no doubt the body was female. But as the train whistle shrilled, a million flies swarmed angrily away from their meal, revealing the body as a mere pulpy red mass, like moist clay shaped into human form. In some places the ravenous mouths of the insects had eaten the flesh down to the bone.

Far off, on the crest of a hill, a line of men and two women clad in robes and coolie hats, looked down at the passing train.

'It must be the girl who set us free,' Alvin croaked as the train plunged into the wood, leaving the horrific scene behind. 'They skinned her alive.'

'Yeah,' Edge agreed softly. 'It's always the woman that flays.'

Chapter Eight

THE scattered remnants of Confederate units fleeing from the scene of pitched battles with advancing Union troops were not uncommon occurrences in the areas immediately behind the war zones.

The surgeon and the young duty officer listened to Hedges' false explanation without suspicion and asked few questions. Their urgent tasks involved the future defence of Chattanooga and past campaigns were of no consequence. Thus, little time was lost in beginning treatment for Hedges and quartering the troopers in a pup tent adjacent to the hospital.

An ether rag plunged Hedges into a deep sleep while the surgeon cleansed his wound of infection and a strong dose of morphine kept him heavily sedated throughout the night. But Forrest allowed the troopers no rest and, in truth, the men would have been reluctant to sleep, despite their fatigue. For a deep-seated fear lurked within each of them. They were sharing quarters with upwards of three thousand Johnnie Rebs and the troopers had only their stolen uniforms to guard their deception. Although it was purely geography that had led them to fight on the union side, they had fought for too long against the Confederates, and suffered too much at their hand, to be able to feel at ease in their present position.

So, following Forrest's instructions, the troopers split into pairs and strolled around the depot section of the camp, taking a mental note of any detail they considered of value in planning its destruction.

Nobody questioned their actions. A number of other, genuine, Rebel soldiers—infantry, cavalry and artillery—were seeking to relieve the boredom of camp life with evening strolls. And there were no signs warning of restricted areas: just stencilled notices on the powder magazines and ammunition stores ordering no smoking in the vicinity.

By the time taps was sounded, the six were back in the privacy of their tent. Lamps were doused and fires died throughout the camp. Only one light flickered: from a candle under a blanket covering the heads of the six troopers crouching in their tent.

Silently, Forrest flattened an area of earth and used a stolen knife to inscribe the area of the depot. Then he carved symbols in several sections, indicating the siting of the various supplies and stores. He passed the knife on to Bell, who added a duplicate set of symbols. And so it went on until Rhett, the last man in the group, had finished making his marks.

Forrest studied the map in the dirt for almost five minutes, committing it to memory and planning a strategy. Finally, he grunted, licked his thumb and forefinger and pinched out the candle flame. He tossed the blanket aside.

'Captain, niggers, guns, powder,' he whispered. 'Let's go.'

136

He pushed his head out through the tent flap and grimaced at the bright moonlight. But it served his purpose in that he could see clearly between the rows of tents and discern no movement—except for the ambling gait of one of the sentries far out on the perimeter. He snaked out and got up into a crouch to scuttle across an area of open ground to the side of the hospital tent. The others imitated his action.

At one end of the hospital there was a canvas porch entrance, but the troopers did not attempt to reach it. They sprawled out full length on the grass and wriggled in under the slack of the side wall. Inside, they stayed down for long moments, listening to the heavy breathing of drugged men. The ward contained a score of cots, twelve of which were occupied by patients. A medic dozed at a paper-littered trestle table beside the flapped entrance.

As Forrest got to his feet and moved stealthily down the aisle between the cots, the others split up to examine the sleeping patients. Seward raised his hand to indicate he had located Hedges and all the men froze, looking towards the sergeant. Forrest halted behind the medic and drew his knife. Suddenly he closed in, clamped his left hand over the man's mouth and used his right to drive the blade deep into the back of the medic. He died with a sigh and was allowed to rest gently across the table top.

Forrest pointed to Bell and Scott, then to a litter resting against the tent wall. Moving like ghosts in the darkness, the designated men lifted the litter and moved down the aisle to Hedges' cot. Within moments the gently snoring Captain had been

137

transferred to the litter and was being carried towards the flap.

Again, Forrest took the lead, peering out of the tent across the quiet camp before slipping outside with the men at his heels. They stayed on their feet this time, but crouched as they ran across the grass to the substantial shadow of the headquarters building. Here, they removed their boots and tied the laces together so the footwear could be slung around their necks.

The road was a dangerously wide strip providing no cover in the silver blueness of the moonlight. They knew there were two sentries at the southern end and had to assume another pair of guards had been posted at the opposite side of the camp. Across it, the looming black shapes of heavy equipment and supply stores were a tempting invitation to the safety of cover.

'Like jack rabbits or snakes?' Seward whispered.

Forrest peered along the road in both directions and could see nothing that moved. He knew that the posted sentries should be looking out at the surrounding hills: but he had been in the army long enough to realise that few soldiers could be relied upon to carry out their duties to the letter. For the hundredth time since he had instituted this mission he cursed the fact that it was not he on the litter, with Hedges calling the shots.

'We move together, in a group,' he rasped softly. 'Slow and easy to keep down the noise. They spot us, run like hell.' He pointed and showed a mirthless grin. 'Like the man said, that way's north.'

'What then?' Rhett asked nervously.

'Then, for Christ's sake, you do your own thinking,' Forrest snarled in low key.

He saw in their gaunt faces that the troopers were no longer neutral. In a situation as tight as this, the sergeant was a bad second best to the sleeping Captain. But Forrest's menacing expression warned against argument and all the men, except the litter bearers, drew their Colts. Their rifles had been left behind in the tent, considered unnecessary encumbrances at this stage.

They stepped out into the soft moonlight, which seemed suddenly brighter and harsher. Forrest took the lead, followed by Bell and Scott with the litter. Seward and Rhett flanked one side, Douglas the other. Their stockinged feet padded silently on the packed down dirt. They looked to neither left nor right and when Forrest stepped into cover, the others scuttled after him.

Forrest grinned his satisfaction. 'How about that?' he muttered.

'You'll make general in no time,' Rhett breathed.

Only Scott heard him.

They were grouped between an ammunition store and a row of supply wagons. Each had some recollection of the map inscribed in the dirt and had some idea of his bearings. But, yet again, no one dared to move until Forrest took the initiative, heading along the line of wagons, then turning between two of them and following the rear fence of the corral. Several horses snorted, sensing the men's presence, but there was no panic among the animals.

The litter was transferred to Seward and Rhett and the group crouched low as the men moved through a cluster of field guns with evil barrels snouting skywards. Next, they went between two lines of timber buildings that could have contained anything—food, maybe, or small arms. The wire-mesh fence at the side of the stockade took on a dull sheen in the moonlight. Forrest raised a hand to call a halt and the men crouched down.

The stockade was about a hundred yards square with a row of low bunkhouses along one side. A bad smell rose from a series of open latrines behind the buildings. The gates were guarded by two men armed with carbines who were bored with their duty. All the slaves were inside the bunkhouses, awesomely aware that to move through the doorways after taps was a crime punishable by death. So the guards squatted on their haunches, shooting craps for match sticks.

'Boots,' Forrest hissed, and the troopers stooped to put on their footwear. 'Billy.'

The youngster stood up, licked his lips and moved out into the open with the sergeant. Forrest spoke softly to him as they approached the stockade gate. The guards heard their footfalls and sprang to their feet, wary of an officer. But when they saw the lack of insignia, they relaxed.

'We ain't due off for another hour,' the younger guard said.

Both men had left their carbines on the ground. Neither wore sidearms.

'You're through right now,' Forrest rasped, and he and Seward drew their revolvers simultaneously. 'Turn around.'

The younger man seemed about to protest, but as

140

Seward pointed the Colt at his eye, he spun around. His companion did likewise. The two troopers stepped up close to the guards and swung their revolvers. As the men crumbled from the blows to the sides of their heads, the troopers caught them and lowered them silently to the ground. Forrest crouched and his knife swung twice. Bloody wounds opened up in both men's chests, left of centre. Seward shot the two bolts on the gate, opened it a crack and slid inside. Forrest went through after him.

There were no fastenings on the doors of the bunkhouses. Both men entered the same building and grimaced as they met the stink of close-packed humanity. Memories of Andersonville flooded their minds, but they pushed all extraneous thoughts from them. Each still had his revolver drawn and raked the interior with it as he allowed his eyes to distend to the darkness. Within moments the double rows of cots took shape and they became aware of at least fifty pairs of eyes watching them fearfully. The stench in the hot, difficult-to-breathe air grew stronger as the slaves sweated their fear.

'Friends,' Forrest whispered. 'Who's head man?'

No answer came. Forrest wanted to bellow for a response, but curbed the impulse.

'No foolin'. Abe Lincoln sent us. You wanna fight for it, you can get free.'

Feet shuffled on the rough timber floor and a massive Negro clad only in filthy, once-white underpants approached the troopers. The whites of his eyes seemed to be luminescent in the murk.

141

'Me head boy in whole stockade. What you want here?'

Forrest spoke to him in low tones, the man listening with deep distrust. He had to take him out across the dangerously open ground of the stockade and show him the dead guards before he could allay suspicion. Only then did the Negro smile and it seemed to be the first expression of joy he had shown in a very long time. Forrest exchanged a few more soft spoken words with him, then beckoned to Seward. The two troopers made good time back to where the others were crouching.

There, the white men watched in an agony of suspense as figures, clad only in ragged Levis, were despatched from the head man's bunkhouse to the others. Then, moments later, in complete silence, more than two hundred slaves loped in single file across the stockade and through the open gate. There they divided, filtering to each side of the supply depot: and sub-divided, splitting into small groups. One such unit was comprised of the head man and four others. They joined the troopers.

'All know must be finished in thirty minutes,' the big man told Forrest. 'Before guard changed.'

Forrest nodded for the Negroes to lead the way. Then they moved off.

Throughout the depot with which they were so familiar, each group reached its objective and started to work with a will they had never possessed before. Doors were swung open with only the smallest of scraping sounds and men flitted inside, to emerge moments later with their burdens.

A group with clips of bullets joined another with

142

a supply of Spencers and Colts. Men weighed down with shot cannisters and cannon balls carried their booty to where other men were sighting artillery pieces. Powder kegs were handed over to men realigning the position of wagons. Four horses were cut out of the corral and harnessed to a wagon in the rear of which Hedges lay sleeping. A dozen liberated slaves loomed around the wagon, loading it with rifles, ammunition and a Gatling gun. Douglas and Scott sat on the box seat, the latter with the reins. Forrest and Seward set up the Gatling. Rhett and Bell—with nothing to do—sweated and jumped at each small sound.

Every trooper knew the deadline was drawing near. The camp on the far side of the road remained peacefully quiet. The perimeter sentries paced up and down in their boredom. The change-of-guard and duty officer dozed in the headquarters building annex.

Then an owl hooted and the grinning face of the head man appeared over the tailgate of the troopers' wagon.

'You count, please,' he whispered to Forrest. 'I never learn.'

Forrest grimaced. Another owl hooted. 'Your boys?'

The head man nodded. 'Must hear this many before all ready.' He raised both hands, fingers splayed, lowered them and raised them again.

'Jesus, that's a lot,' Seward rasped.

'Too damn many,' Forrest snarled. Another bird call sounded. He pulled his knife and made a slit in the canvas on the left hand side of the wagon. He

143

swivelled the Gatling so that its muzzle snouted through the slit. 'There just can't be that many birds awake around here.'

Three hoots sounded together.

'How many more?' the Negro asked politely.

An owl call sounded. A shot rang out.

'That's it!' Forrest lied, and raised his voice to a yell. 'Let's go, Johnnie!'

Scott cracked the whip and slapped the reins. The wagon leapt forward and Bell and Rhett gripped Hedges' arms to keep him from being flung across the wagon bed.

Shouts sounded from every section of the camp as men scrambled from their tents and gave vent to their confusion. A score of cannon roared and rained body-mangling death on a distant area. A score of Negroes strained their sheened backs against four wagons and the vehicles trundled across the road trailing flaring fuses. Rifle, pistol and rapid Gatling fire peppered the night with deadly sound.

As the duty officer and guard ran from the head-quarters building two men fell beneath the crushing wheels of a wagon and chunks of flesh were scattered hundreds of yards under the impact of a violent explosion. The wagon and half the building disintegrated, raining burning timber and tongues of flame on to men and canvas. The three other mobile bombs rumbled into the camp and their searing explosions turned a dozen running figures into human torches.

Cries of agony ripped across the angry roar of spreading flames. A naked soldier stared in disbelief at his twisted leg, lying ten yards from where he sat.

144

Then his head exploded under the impact of a burst of Gatling fire.

The terrified sentries on the depot perimeter rushed forward, firing blindly. A Negro crouching beside a powder magazine, took a bullet in the head and fell forward. The match in his hand raked across timber and flared. It dropped into the prepared fuse trailing through the open doorway. Seconds sliced away at time and the building exploded with an ear-splitting roar. Thirty Negroes and four guards in the vicinity were either charred to cinders or torn limb from limb.

Naked and half-dressed soldiers, unable to hear the orders of their officers against the din of gunfire and screaming, rushed among the tents in panic, shooting indiscriminately towards the road. More than one Rebel fell wounded or dead, shot in the back by a comrade.

The wagon carrying the Union troopers reached the road and made a slithering, lock-wheeled right turn. As Scott crouched low on the seat, lashing the team, Douglas pumped rifle fire into the camp. Then, with Seward feeding the hopper, Forrest opened up with the Gatling gun.

Answering fire pecked at the speeding wagon from both sides, the Rebels aiming at it, the Negroes firing to the front, rear and under it. Soon the side on the left was a mass of splintered wood and the canvas was peppered with holes.

A second salvo of cannon fire roared. The thump of metal against flesh and the ground gave rise to a new crescendo of screaming. Then improvised battlecries and the thunder of hoofbeats added to the din.

Delirious with the joy of freedom attained amid such revenge, scores of bellowing Negroes poured on to the road, running at full tilt and galloping bareback on stolen horses. They streamed in the wake of the racing wagon, firing wildly as they went. Answering fire brought down riders, runners and horses. Coal black bodies pitched to the ground to feed it with their blood.

The wagon hurtled through the opening in the perimeter at the north end of the road and the less than sixty survivors among the freed slaves dashed out after it. A rattle of rifle fire followed them.

Then two more powder magazines exploded with gigantic roars which sent heat waves swirling across the entire camp. Ammunition stored in two buildings was destroyed in a series of minor, chattering explosions.

Forrest, Seward, Rhett and Bell looked back down the road as the wagon slowed on the incline out of the valley. The whole depot side of the camp was engulfed in smoke-billowing flames while a score of lesser blades dotted the area of the soldiers' quarters. In the flickering firelight, men ran in every direction, or stumbled about in a daze. Against this backdrop of death and destruction the Negroes on horseback halted their animals so that their fellows on foot could swing up. The gunfire from the camp had ceased, as had the battlecries of the freed slaves. For each had taken time to look back along the road: to see the gruesome spectacle of twisted and bloodied bodies that littered the way to freedom.

146

In the rear of the wagon, Hedges moaned and stirred, but the morphine held him prisoner to his sleep.

'We sure gave 'em hell, didn't we, Frank?' Seward said in high excitement, drinking in the sight of the carnage before the wagon crested a rise and all he could see was the orange hue doming the sky above the valley.

Bell stabbed a finger at Hedges. 'You reckon he'll ever believe what we did?'

Forrest spat over the tailgate of the wagon, watching the Negroes streaming over the hillcrest behind. 'Reckon he will,' the sergeant replied. 'He'll have it in black and white.'

The wagon and its strange escort rumbled into the night, every yard travelled taking them a yard closer to safety.

*   *   *

MOST of the hostages left the freight train at Salt Lake City to transfer to the comfort of passenger cars but Edge, Alvin and Beth, with no facilities for raising the fare, stayed aboard: until Cheyenne where there was a change-over of crews.

Both the new engineer and his fireman were company men who worked by the book: and the book said no passengers on freight trains—especially no passengers without the price of a ticket. Sheriff Bodie, two deputies and a quartet of railroad officers backed up the order. With the former crewmen nowhere in sight, neither Edge nor the couple even attempted to explain their situation.

They were escorted outside the town limits.

147

Edge, weaponless apart from the razor, accepted the treatment philosophically. Beth was incensed by the bum's rush. Alvin asked how far it was to Deadwood in the Dakotas, because his mother's brother ran a saloon up there.

It was a long way, across the south-east corner of Wyoming and the north-west segment of Nebraska. For no better reason than it was a place to aim for, Edge went with the runaways.

At first they walked but then, with the tacit approval of Alvin and Beth, Edge stole a wagon and two horses from a farm. Edge waited impatiently while the conscience-stricken Alvin scrawled an unsigned IOU in the dirt outside the barn door.

Food and water were plentiful along the route and they made good time. But in the malicious emptiness of the Dakota Badlands their luck ran out. One of the horses broke a leg in a gopher hole. The following morning, as the second of the pair was grazing, it was spooked by a snake and bolted.

After a full morning's walk, fighting a biting north wind the whole way, they entered a small village peopled by dirt farmers. Strangers were not common in the area and always viewed with suspicion.

The dour-faced saloon keeper, who had rooms for rent, demanded payment in advance and backed them out with a shotgun when their poverty became obvious.

'What now?' Alvin asked wearily as they moved down the only street in the village.

He was holding the arm of Beth, but she was giving him more support than he to her. Both were tired, hungry and struggling against a depression which threatened to drop them in their tracks.

Edge's hooded eyes raked the street on both sides, unwilling to berate the whim that had brought him to this God forsaken spot. Instead, he reasoned that he had chosen to come, and all that mattered was finding an answer to his immediate problem.

He spotted a shack on the edge of the village, crudely built and badly maintained. A wooden sign on the roof proclaimed: SHERIFF. But it was not this lettering which attracted him; caused him to alter direction and angle across to the decrepit law office.

To one side of the door was a board nailed to the wall, and a half dozen wanted notices were thumb-tacked to it. All of them were yellowed by age and weather and one of the oldest showed a picture of a young man in the uniform of an army captain. The faded lettering beneath was as familiar to him as the face depicted on the poster:

WANTED
FOR THE MURDER OF WAR
VETERAN ELLIOT THOMBS
former captain J. C. Hedges

Beneath this, scrawled in charcoal, was the additional information:

$100 REWARD

Edge moved along to the window and a grin spread across his face as he peered inside and saw a bearded, pot-bellied man in his fifties sleeping soundly in a swivel chair at the desk.

Alvin and Beth looked at him oddly as he returned to them, unable to comprehend the reason for the cold grin. He spoke softly to them and Alvin seemed to greet every word with an emphatic shake of his head. But, after a dispirited glance around at the unfriendly cluster of buildings and the harshness of the surrounding countryside, Beth gave a nod of approval.

Out-voted, anxious to please the woman, Alvin fell in with the plan. He bunched his fist in his jacket pocket, simulating the bulge of a gun, and followed Edge back across the street towards the law office. Beth hurried ahead, tore down the wanted poster and pushed open the door. The sound of footfalls in the office jerked the sheriff from sleep.

'What—?'

Beth held out the poster and dropped it on the dusty desk. 'It says a hundred dollars for him,' she cut in. 'He's the one.'

The sheriff stood up, squinting at Edge, obviously not connecting the leathery-faced prisoner with the youthful reproduction on the poster. But he drew one of the two six-guns holstered at his hips.

'That's Hedges?' he asked.

'Lot of blood's flowed since I looked like that,' Edge said easily, his narrowed eyes moving from the perplexed face of the sheriff, to the safe in one corner, the barred door of an empty cell in the other.

Alvin was nervous, trembling before his own conscience. Not so Beth. She was experienced in the

150

harsh realities of life on the wrong side of the tracks. She smiled beguilingly at the lawman.

'Hundred dollars, sheriff,' she reminded softly. 'Then my fiance will help you lock him up.' She looked at Edge venomously. 'He's a real mean bastard.'

Alvin gasped at the profanity as Beth tried to bite back the word. The sheriff looked from Edge to the swells of Beth's breasts.

'Yes, ma'am. You did your duty and you're entitled to the reward.'

He came out from behind the desk and moved sideways to the safe.

'You keep him covered now, young feller,' he urged, then turned and fitted a key into the lock on the safe. He swung the door wide. Then he began to count out a wad of five dollar bills, still holding the Remington revolver in one hand.

Edge moved on the balls of his feet and reached the sheriff in three strides. A floorboard creaked just as Edge's hand grasped the butt of the holstered gun.

Beth gasped and the sheriff whirled. His face was painted with fear. His finger tightened on the trigger and the Remington leapt, spitting flame. The woman did not live long enough to scream. The bullet angled in through her jaw and tunnelled the roof of her mouth up to her brain. Alvin darted forward and caught her dead body in his arms.

'Drop it, sheriff!' Edge rasped, pressing the Remington against the lawman's temple.

The matching weapon clattered to the floor as the sheriff straightened, staring at the dead woman with dazed eyes. Edge scooped up the gun and snatched the sheaf of bills from the limp hand.

Alvin looked with wide, tear-bloated eyes at the blood coursing down Beth's chest to channel into the valley between her breasts. Horror etched deep lines in his young face.

'She's dead,' he said incredulously, as if he had to convince himself of this truth.

Edge looked at the sheriff through narrowed eyes. 'Where'd they bury whores around here?' he asked.

All along the street, doors and windows were slammed closed. The inhabitants of the village were learning once more that you could not trust strangers in the Badlands.

The sheriff was deeply afraid, aware he could expect no help from the citizens, who paid him to protect them.

'She wasn't a whore,' Alvin challenged with a sob, cradling her head. 'That was all behind her.'

'Sheriff?' Edge insisted.

The man gulped. 'Everyone gets buried out of town aways. Out in the hills. Place called Wounded Knee.'

Edge nodded and peeled two five dollar bills from the roll. He held them out towards the kid. 'Here.'

Alvin accepted the money unthinkingly, then came out of his daze with a start. His eyes were full of hurt as he watched Edge go to the door. 'This won't get me far,' he accused.

'Ain't for you,' Edge told him. 'It'll get her where she's goin'. Six feet—straight down. Ought to cover it.'

'For the funeral!' the kid exclaimed as realisation

hit him and he began to shed tears onto the dead face of the woman.

'Right,' Edge confirmed. 'To bury your tart at Wounded Knee.'

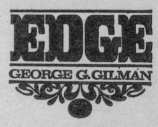

HANNIE CAULDER, by William Terry. A damn good book and great movie. The story of a woman who takes to the gun to avenge her husband. Hannie Caulder is a pioneer woman. She and her husband Jim run a relay station near the Mexican border. She's a gorgeous hunk of female—*picture* Raquel Welch —and a good woman. One day the three Clemens brothers ride up to the Caulder place. The Clemens are drunk and in a blind rage because they've just bungled a bank heist. Jim Caulder is brutally killed and his Hannie is then subjected to an incredible ordeal of violence, rape and sadism. She's left for dead. Now the real story begins, and we won't spoil an exciting and different western by telling you more.   **P94—95¢**

GOLD WAGON, by Chet Cunningham. A helluva tough and gritty novel of men after gold. It was a deadly game, with a ton of gold to the winner. The men at war were hungry and desperate, nothing seemed to be able to stop them from chasing their prize. Soldiers of the U.S. Army were massacred, mere lawmen were disregarded or intimidated. Was there no way to protect a shipment of gold bullion—400 lb. bars—even as big a quantity as a ton of it? One man, Jim Steel, had an idea. He was an ex-lawman, but he wasn't above taking a chance on the treasure of a lifetime.   **P96—95¢**

BOUNTY HUNT AT BALLARAT, by Clayton Matthews. A western in the best hard-hitting tradition! When Clint Devlin rode into Ballarat, he thought he was coming to avenge the brutal murder of his girlfriend's father. And he thought that the murderer was a woman. He was wrong. But it took a while to find out the truth. And the truth surprised everyone. Especially Clint Devlin. *Bounty Hunt at Ballarat* is a tense Western drama, with just a little something added.   **P178—95¢**